LISA THOMPSON

worked as a radio broadcast assistant first at the BBC and then for an independent production company making plays and comedy programmes. She grew up in Essex and now lives in Suffolk with her family.

The Goldfish Boy was one of the bestselling debuts of 2017 and was shortlisted for a number of prizes, including the Waterstones Children's Book Prize. Her stunning second book, *The Light Jar*, was chosen as the Children's Book of the Week in *The Times*, the *Guardian* and the *Observer* on publication, and *The Day I Was Erased* was Children's Book of the Week in *The Times*.

For my editor, Lauren Fortune.

First published in the UK as *The Graveyard Riddle* by Scholastic, 2021
This edition published as *The Magpie Riddle*, 2025
Scholastic, Bosworth Avenue, Warwick, CV34 6UQ
Scholastic Ireland, 89E Lagan Road, Dublin Industrial Estate, Glasnevin, Dublin, D11 HP5F

SCHOLASTIC and associated logos are trademarks and/or
registered trademarks of Scholastic Inc.

Text © Lisa Thompson, 2021.
Cover and inside illustrations © Mike Lowery, 2021, 2025.
The moral rights of the author and illustrator have been asserted by them.

ISBN 978 0702 34428 2

A CIP catalogue record for this book is available from the British Library.

All rights reserved.
This book is sold subject to the condition that it shall not, by way of trade or otherwise,
be lent, hired out or otherwise circulated in any form of binding or cover other than
that in which it is published. No part of this publication may be reproduced, stored in a
retrieval system, or transmitted in any form or by any other means (electronic, mechanical,
photocopying, recording or otherwise) or used to train any artificial intelligence
technologies without prior written permission of Scholastic Limited. Subject to EU law
Scholastic Limited expressly reserves this work from the text and data mining exception.

Printed in the UK
Paper made from wood grown in sustainable forests and other controlled sources.

10 9 8 7 6 5 4 3 2 1

This is a work of fiction. Any resemblance to actual people, events or locales is entirely
coincidental.

www.scholastic.co.uk

For safety or quality concerns:
UK: www.scholastic.co.uk/productinformation
EU: www.scholastic.ie/productinformation

THE MAGPIE RIDDLE

A GOLDFISH BOY MYSTERY

LISA THOMPSON

SCHOLASTIC

CHAPTER 1

Frankie is a conker-brown dachshund and a very wise little dog. For example, I take him for a walk every day after school and at weekends and he always turns left out of our driveway. He knows *exactly* which way to go: the graveyard.

This afternoon was like any other. We curved around the semicircle of houses at the bottom of Chestnut Close and came to an alleyway. Frankie stopped to sniff at a patch of weeds. Sometimes I wondered if he was actually smelling something good, or pretending so that he could have a rest. His legs were really little, after all.

"Come on, Frankie. Let's go," I said. He shook himself and we set off again.

Some people thought I was weird because I liked going to the graveyard. To them, a graveyard is creepy. It makes them think of spooky things like rotten corpses and wailing ghosts. I don't feel like that at all. To me it's full of colour and light and wildlife. In fact, it's probably my favourite place in the world.

We came out of the alleyway and I took a long, deep breath. A gentle breeze moved through the trees making a soft *shhh* sound as warm, yellow dots of sunlight danced across the headstones. When Dad lived with us I used to go to the graveyard when he and Mum started arguing. There was no shouting there. It was always peaceful.

As we walked along the pathway Frankie stopped in mid-trot and began to sniff at the air. His long, brown ears flapped gently in the wind as he searched for the scent he'd picked up.

"What is it, Frankie?" I said. "Can you smell the souls of the dead people?" I looked down at the headstone beside us. It read:

Benjamin Henry Brady
Born 31st July 1884
Died 27th January 1954

Frankie's wet, brown nose wriggled. I knew that a dog's sense of smell was forty times stronger than ours. Could Frankie smell Benjamin Brady's aftershave, still lingering in the air? He sniffed a few more times and then pulled on his lead. He was ready to carry on.

We passed the large horse chestnut tree which had a circular bench around its trunk and the rusty tap where visitors could fill their watering cans. We usually stayed on the main pathway, headed towards the church and then took a loop back to where we started, but just past the tap I spotted a track we hadn't used for a while. It was overgrown with a tangle of ivy and brambles and led to the oldest part of the graveyard. No mourners visited that part any more. They were all dead and buried themselves.

"Let's go this way for a change, shall we, Frankie?" I said. My little dog sat down on the pathway, confused that we weren't going on our usual route.

"Come on, it's not far," I said.

The track soon became thick with weeds and I had to trample them down so that we could get through. Surrounding us were ancient headstones, peeking at us through the undergrowth like grey ships bobbing on a sea of green. Some were speckled with bright splashes of orange lichen, as though they'd been splattered with paint.

I carried on walking but a vicious-looking bramble caught my ankle. It drew blood and I took a tissue out of my school blazer pocket and pressed it against the scratch. After a few seconds it stopped.

Frankie sneezed. He was almost buried in weeds.

"Maybe this wasn't such a good idea after all," I said. "Come on, let's head back."

I scooped Frankie under my arm, stood up and then stopped. Beyond the track was an old red-brick wall which circled the perimeter of the graveyard. Part of the wall had crumbled away and there was now a V-shaped gap in the middle. I didn't remember noticing it before.

"I wonder what's through there?" I said. I took a few careful steps, checking for more brambles and crushing any nettles under foot. The pathway stopped so I had to walk in between the actual graves where the ground was uneven. When we got to the crumbling wall I put Frankie down. He gave himself a shake and sniffed at the air. Through the gap I could make out some windows and a door.

"It's a house!" I said.

We scrambled over the pile of bricks and found ourselves in knee-deep grass. In front of us was a cottage. It had a crooked doorway in the centre with four small, black-framed windows, a wonky roof and a chimney. It looked a bit like a toddler's painting of a house. The once-white walls were now dirty-grey with patches of green, slimy moss. The roof had missing tiles and a deep overhang that almost hid the windows. It must be very dark inside. Beyond the house was another brick wall. It was as if it had been deliberately hidden from view.

"Isn't it incredible, Frankie?" I said. "I never knew this was here. A secret house!" Frankie was busy snuffling around at all the new smells. I waded through the grass and peered through the downstairs window. The glass was cracked in the corner and thick with dirt, as though a curtain had been drawn on the inside.

Frankie began to pull on his lead. A blackbird was stabbing at a patch of soil with its bright orange beak. It stopped to watch us for a few seconds, then carried on, deciding that we were not much of a threat. The door to the house was dark green and slightly ajar. I hesitated for a second, then gave the door a nudge with my knee. It didn't move. I leaned my shoulder against it and shoved hard a few times.

Very slowly the door inched open until there was enough space to squeeze through. I peered inside. There was no way anyone was living here. Surely there was no harm in taking a look?

"Come on," I said to Frankie. "Let's go inside."

We walked into a small, square room with a low ceiling. It was dark and I had to wait for my eyes to adjust to the gloom before I looked around. The room was empty apart from an open fireplace filled with rubble, and a wooden chair covered with a thick layer of dust. It smelled musty and damp, a bit like the smell in the kitchen cupboard underneath our sink.

"Wow," I said, turning around. "I wonder how long it's been since anyone lived here?" Frankie sniffed at the dusty wooden floor and sneezed. Against a wall was a wooden staircase with no handrail and a lot of missing steps.

"I guess we won't be going up there anytime soon," I said. I could just make out two doorways at the top.

There was another room downstairs and Frankie pulled me towards it. This room was much the same: dusty, dark and very bare. I walked over to the window. On the windowsill was a round pebble. I picked it up. It was cold and smooth, like a tiny egg.

"I wonder where this came from?" I said. I put it back, then wiped a small, clean circle in the dirty glass with my hand. Through it I could see the gap in the crumbling wall, the tops of the headstones and the newer graves near the main pathway.

"I can't wait to tell Matthew about this place!" I said to Frankie. "I bet he never knew this was here, either." Matthew Corbin was my best friend and lived in the house opposite mine on Chestnut Close.

I checked my watch and decided to head home as Mum would have dinner ready soon. I turned to go, when I heard something. A slow, creaking noise coming from upstairs. It sounded like someone was moving very carefully across the floorboards. I looked up at the ceiling, listening hard.

"I think there's somebody upstairs," I whispered. I held tightly on to Frankie's lead and we walked slowly back to the first room and towards the broken stairs. I peered up, terrified that a face might suddenly appear at the top. The creaking sound stopped.

"H-hello?" I called. "Is someone there?" I listened, but there was no reply. All I could hear was the breeze rustling through the long grass outside. That must have been it – the wind blowing through the cracks in the windows, making the floorboards creak. Frankie growled.

"There's nothing there, Frankie. It's just the wind," I said. "Come on, let's go."

I hurried back to the door and we squeezed through the gap. When we were out in the long grass, I turned and tugged on the door to try and shut it. It wouldn't budge.

That's when I spotted something across the top of the doorframe. I took a step back. There were words scratched into the dark wood. I felt a shiver tingle down my spine to the soles of my feet as I read what it said.

"LORD, HAVE MERCY UPON US."

CHAPTER 2

I still had goose bumps as Frankie and I walked back through the graveyard. Who had scratched those words into the wood above the cottage door? They sounded ominous. The whole place made me nervous.

I was still thinking about it when I came out of the alleyway on to Chestnut Close. Old Nina was in her front garden, trying to reach a crisp bag that had blown under a shrub near her door. Her tabby cat, Pepper, was sitting on her step and blinking in the sun. Old Nina had got Pepper as a kitten last summer and she had turned out to be very shy and timid, just like her owner. The cat took one look at me and Frankie and darted inside.

"Would you like me to get that for you, Nina?" I said.

"Oh, if it's no trouble, Melody," she said. "If I kneel down I might not be able to get back up again." Old Nina always looked smart and today she was wearing a light-green blouse with black trousers. Pinned to her blouse was a blue brooch in the shape of a daisy. She wore it every day and it twinkled in the sunlight. I reached for the crisp bag and she took it from me.

"Sometimes the wind does like to blow in the wrong direction, don't you think?" said Old Nina, with a smile.

I didn't know how she did it, but Old Nina always made a simple sentence sound really meaningful. As she smiled I noticed a web of tiny red lines on her cheeks. Mum said she thought Old Nina was nearly a hundred years old, but no one really knew. Her house was called the Rectory and it sat right at the bottom of our dead-end street, next to the alleyway. It had stood there for many, many years and long before our boring, beige houses were built. I wondered whether Old Nina might know something about the strange cottage.

"Nina, do you know anything about a little

house on the edge of the graveyard?" I said. "It's really rundown. I don't think anyone has lived there for years."

As Old Nina thought she scrunched the crisp bag in her hand. Her skin was paper-thin.

"Do you mean the old plague house?" said Old Nina. "Was it behind a red-brick wall?"

"Yes!" I said. "What's a plague house?"

Old Nina pressed her lips together.

"It's not very nice I'm afraid," she said. "People who had been infected with the plague were kept there to try and stop the disease spreading. This was hundreds of years ago, of course, when our town was just a village. My Arthur did some research when he was alive."

Arthur was Old Nina's husband and he used to be the vicar in the church. He died long before I was born.

"Plague houses were often built close to churches. Some parts of the house date back to the seventeenth century, I believe," Old Nina said. "Although most of it was rebuilt in later years."

"That's incredible," I said. "I thought it was old but I didn't realize it was *that* old. Why did they build a wall round it?"

"Maybe the churchgoers wanted to stop being reminded of it as it has such a sad history," she said. "I think the wall went up in Victorian times."

I couldn't wait to tell Matthew about the house. He loved interesting facts, just like me.

A dog started yapping and we both turned to look at number seven.

"Oh dear. It looks like our chatting has set that puppy off again," said Old Nina. "Anyway, it's nice to see you, Melody." She slowly made her way to her front steps where Pepper had returned, waiting to greet her.

Rory and Hannah Jenkins and their baby, Max, lived at number seven, and standing at their windowsill was their white, fluffy dog called Wilson. They'd only had Wilson for a few weeks and barking at the neighbours through the window seemed to be his favourite hobby. His barking became more intense when he spotted Frankie. Frankie merely glanced at him and yawned.

I crossed the road to our house, number three.

"Melody! Can you give me a hand?" called Mum as soon as I closed our front door.

"Just a minute!" I called back. I unhooked Frankie's lead and he trotted off to the kitchen, his pointed tail tick-tocking like a clock's pendulum. I went into the dining room and Mum was holding a huge mirror in her arms against the wall. Her face was squashed against the glass as she struggled to hold it upright.

"Mum! You should have waited for me!" I said. I hurried over to help her.

"I thought I'd hang it up, but I can't see what I'm doing," she said.

I slipped my hand around the back of the mirror and hooked the chain on to the nail.

"You can let go now," I said.

Mum carefully eased the mirror down, straightened it, then took a step back.

"Fantastic!" she said. "I've been meaning to put that up for months. Doesn't that look better? It makes the room feel so much bigger! High five, Team MC!"

I slapped Mum's hand, even though it was a bit cringy. After Dad left, Mum started calling us Team MC after our names: Melody and Claudia. But even though I didn't really like the name, she was right. We *had* become a team. The two of us took on all the jobs that Dad used to do, like fitting a flat-pack chest of drawers together and unplumbing our broken washing machine and taking it to the recycling centre. We'd even wallpapered the lounge after watching a video on YouTube.

I looked around at the dining room.

"Where have all our photos gone?" I said. Our side cabinet was usually covered with framed pictures; there were a few of me as a baby, one of Mum outside the organic café where she worked, Frankie as a puppy, Frankie wearing a Santa hat, the three of us on the beach where Frankie spent all day digging holes in the sand.

"I'm having a declutter," said Mum. "It looks nicer with everything a bit clearer, don't you think?" A cardboard box filled with the framed photos was on the floor and she pushed the box with her foot so it slid under the sideboard. Our table, usually covered with books, magazines and paperwork, had also been cleared. In the middle was a slim glass vase filled with cream flowers. She'd clearly been busy.

"How was your walk?" said Mum. I followed her to the kitchen.

"Amazing!" I said. "I found this old house! Well, it's more of a cottage really. Nina said it was a plague house!"

"That's nice," said Mum, flicking through some post that was on the side. I could tell she wasn't listening. She'd been like that for a few weeks now. She clearly had something on her mind, but whenever I asked what was wrong, she said "nothing". I'd also noticed that she'd been getting a lot of post marked "PRIVATE" and "URGENT". They looked like bills.

"I'm going to go and see Matthew," I said, following her to the kitchen. I couldn't wait to tell him about my graveyard discovery.

"OK. Dinner will be ready in about twenty minutes," said Mum. She put one of the envelopes marked "URGENT" to one side without opening it.

Matthew lived at number nine and he'd been my best friend for nearly a year now. People used to think he was strange because he didn't like to go outside. What they didn't realize is that he had an extreme fear of germs so going outside was pretty traumatic for him. He thought germs were everywhere, ready to dig under his skin or crawl up his nose and make him or his family really ill. He got so bad that he stopped going to school and started wearing plastic gloves all the time. But last summer his parents took him to see a therapist called Dr Rhodes once a week and he's been getting a bit better ever since.

Oh, and he solved a mystery. A toddler called Teddy went missing from Chestnut Close and Matthew worked out what had happened because he was always just watching the neighbours from the window. It was huge news for a while and we even had TV news crews on the street! Teddy was found safe. Although I think most people have forgotten about it now.

I pushed the doorbell of number nine and waited. Immediately, Wilson reappeared on the windowsill of number seven and started yapping again. His breath made a small circle of mist on the glass. Matthew's mum, Sheila, opened the door.

"Oh hello, Melody, love. Did you want Matthew?" she said.

"Hi, Sheila!" I said. "Yes please."

"MATTHEW!! IT'S MELODY!" yelled Sheila, towards their conservatory. "Listen to that dog. You'd think he'd be worn out by now, wouldn't you? Drives me mad."

She rolled her eyes and I grinned back at her. Sheila is lovely. Matthew appeared behind her, holding a pool cue.

"Ah, here he is," said Sheila. "We're leaving in ten minutes, Matthew. OK? I'll see you later, Melody. Give my love to your mum."

Matthew rested the base of the cue on the doormat and gripped the top. His dad, Brian, had bought a pool table ages ago to try and encourage him downstairs. He had just started using it.

"All right?" he said.

"Hi, Matthew!" I said. "You'll never guess what I found in the graveyard! In the old part, right behind a wall there's this—"

Jake Bishop from number five appeared in the hallway behind him. He was also holding a pool cue.

"Oh, hi, Jake," I said. "I didn't know you were here." I looked at Matthew but he was staring at the cue and twisting it in his hands.

Wilson's yapping was getting louder by the second. Jake jumped down on to the path beside me.

"I wish that little rat would shut up," he said. "It's all we hear all day long. Yap, yap yap. And if it's not the rat then that ugly baby is yelling its head off."

Jake's house was attached to the Jenkins's so they probably heard everything through the adjoining wall, including Max crying.

Matthew stepped down on to the path and joined Jake. He was just wearing socks, no shoes. He'd never have stepped outside wearing just socks a few months ago. He would have been too worried about the germs. We all watched Wilson. Every time he barked, he did a little jump.

"Here, Jake," said Matthew. "Wilson looks like he's been in a washing machine on spin, doesn't he?" This cracked Jake up.

"Yeah!" said Jake. "He looks like a wig on legs!"

"He's a Bichon Frise. He's *supposed* to be fluffy," I said. "Don't tease him!" But Matthew and Jake both ignored me.

Jake used to be pretty horrible to Matthew and called him a weirdo when he spotted him in his window. But ever since last summer when Teddy went missing, they'd become friends.

Wilson must have run out of energy as he stopped barking and just sat there, panting. He then gave the window a lick, leaving a slimy smear. Matthew stepped back up into the house.

Jake followed him inside, then he turned to face me. "Melody, you should put Frankie next to Wilson and then they'll look like sausage and mash!" he said.

Matthew threw his head back and let out the loudest laugh I'd heard him do in ages. Jake laughed too. I stood there, feeling invisible.

"Come on, let's finish this game before we go," said Jake. He walked off towards a conservatory at the back of the house. That's where the pool table was.

"Are you going out?" I asked.

Matthew stared at the ground.

"Yeah. Mum is taking us to the cinema. It's a kind of treat for all the work I've been doing at therapy," he said. He didn't look at me.

"That's nice," I said. I felt a lump forming in my throat as I swallowed.

"Anyway, what were you saying? About something in the graveyard?" said Matthew.

He looked up at me then, blinking through his long fringe.

"It doesn't matter," I said. "You'd better get back to your game if you're going out soon. I'll see you later, Matthew."

"Bye, Melody."

The door closed behind me before I'd even reached the pavement.

CHAPTER 3

The next day when I came out of school, I spotted the top of Matthew's head as he stood by the gates. He was waiting for a gap in the crowd. Matthew always liked to have space around him. I sometimes thought that he was a bit like a magnet but the wrong way around, pushing everyone away. The mass of students eased off a little and he quickly ducked out and headed down the street. I ran to catch him up.

"Hi, Matthew! How was the cinema?" I said, trotting along beside him.

"Good," he said. He kept his head down, walking really fast. Before we became friends, I used to think he walked quickly to get away from me. Now I knew it was so he got home sooner. I think being at school all day was tiring when he was battling with the thought of germs in his head.

"Did Jake have a nice time too?" I said.

Matthew nodded. "Yeah, I think so," he said.

We walked in silence for a while.

"Hey, do you fancy going to the graveyard later?" I said. "I've found this incredible building that Old Nina said used to be a plague house!"

"A what?" said Matthew.

"A plague house!" I said. "It was a place to keep infected people so they wouldn't spread the disease to others. Imagine it! Being locked away with all the sick people. Knowing you probably weren't ever going to get out alive."

Matthew shuddered. "Dunno if I want to see *that*," he said.

Someone cycled up behind us and skidded to a halt. I turned around to tell them to get on to the road and saw it was Jake.

"You do realize that you shouldn't be cycling on the pavement, don't you?" I said.

"Er, yeah," he said. "And?" He pulled the handlebars up and did a wheelie. The bike thumped back down and just missed my foot.

"Watch it!" I said. Jake could be such an idiot

sometimes. Matthew marched off quickly, leaving us both behind.

"What's the matter with him?" said Jake.

"He wants to get home," I said. "Maybe going to the cinema last night has made him anxious."

Jake snorted.

"Nah. He's over all that 'Goldfish Boy' stuff now," he said.

I sighed. Matthew was known as the "Goldfish Boy" for a while. Two kids staying next door to him had started calling him that, saying he looked like a goldfish in a tank when he looked out of the window.

"It's not a case of 'getting over it', Jake," I said. "It can take months or even years to undo how your brain thinks."

"Yeah, well," said Jake. "I think he just wants to get away from you, Melody Bird."

"What?" I said.

Jake smirked and wiped his nose on the back of his hand. His wrist was red and cracked with eczema. Jake was allergic to loads of stuff and it looked like something had caused a flare up.

"See ya later, Melody," he said. He bumped his bike down the kerb and sped off.

I watched Matthew's school bag bang against his

back as he paced along. Was he really trying to avoid me? I hurried to catch him up.

"So, do you want to come and see the plague house then?" I said. "It's got something scratched on the door frame."

"Has it? What does it say?" said Matthew. I *knew* he'd be interested.

"It says, 'Lord Have Mercy Upon Us'," I said. "Spooky, isn't it?"

Matthew smiled slightly.

"They used to put red crosses on the doors too," he said. "To warn villagers that there were infected people inside."

I grinned. "We could see if there's a cross still there! Or the remains of one at least," I said.

Matthew scrunched up his nose and took a long breath. "I don't think so, Melody," he said.

I suppose it was a big ask getting someone with a fear of germs to visit a plague house, even if the plague was long gone by now. We turned down our road. There were only seven houses in Chestnut Close and hardly any traffic so it was always quiet. I spotted something outside the house right next to mine. It was a bright purple FOR SALE sign on top of a white, wooden post.

"Matthew! Look!" I said. "Number one have put their house up for sale."

"Oh yeah," said Matthew. "I guess it's been empty for a while now."

We carried on walking but as we got closer, Matthew stopped.

"Hang on a minute, Melody," he said. "That's not number one. That's *your* house. Your house is for sale!"

CHAPTER 4

I paced around the lounge as Frankie sat by the couch, watching me go back and forth across the carpet. Mum wasn't home from work yet. I kept checking the driveway as if that would make her appear quicker.

For sale? Our house? There must be a mistake! I was tempted to ring the number on the board and tell them they had put the sign up in the wrong garden and it should be in next door's garden, at number one. But something stopped me. What if they said I was wrong?

I went to the kitchen and walked around there a few times. Any second now, Mum would come in looking as shocked as I felt, saying that there had been a mix up. She'd call the estate agent; the sign would be moved and everything would go back to normal.

But then I noticed something else. The shelves in the kitchen were usually piled high with junk mail, recipe books, keys and loose change. Now the shelves were clear and our stuff had been replaced with three glass jars filled with dried pasta.

I felt my stomach slowly twist into a tight knot as the reality of what was going on began to dawn on me. Mum hadn't been decluttering so the house looked nice for us – she had been tidying up so that the house was ready to sell! Frankie trotted into the kitchen.

"Oh Frankie. What's happening?" I said. I picked him up and gave him a squeeze.

A car pulled on to our driveway. I waited. Then I heard Mum fumbling with her keys and the front door flew open.

"Melody! Melody? It's not as bad as it looks, I promise!" she called out. She came into the kitchen. I put Frankie down on the floor and he trotted over to greet her.

"I'm so sorry, Melody. I didn't realize the estate agent was going to put a sign up today," she said.

I felt the air rush out of my lungs. It wasn't a mistake. She took a step towards me but I stepped back.

"I wanted to talk to you first," she said. "It all happened a bit faster than I was expecting."

"What about 'Team MC', Mum? What about us always being in everything together?" I said. "I don't want to move!"

Mum's face fell. "Let me explain. We can't afford to stay here any more – it's just too expensive. But we can find somewhere else, somewhere really special."

"What are you talking about?" I said. "This is our home!"

"I know, but we have to face facts," said Mum. "Let's have a look at some properties on the laptop later, shall we? There are some lovely places out there."

"Oh, so you've been looking already, have you? Without me?" I said. "How could you have lied to me, Mum? How could you not have told me? Especially after what Dad did! You're ... you're just as bad as him!"

Mum looked like she'd been slapped. I knew what I said would hurt her. After all, Dad was the biggest liar we had ever known. She took her jacket off and put it on the back of the kitchen chair.

"I didn't lie to you, Melody – I was just waiting for the right moment to tell you. But it's the truth. We've *got* to find somewhere cheaper to live."

"No!" I said. "You can't do this, Mum. You can't force me to move!" I suddenly thought of something. "You've *got* to get in touch with Dad. If he knew we were struggling to afford to live here then he'd *help*."

Mum stared down at the floor. "We don't need him, Melody," she said. "He made his choice."

I recognized the steely determination in her voice. That's how she had sounded in the weeks after Dad had left. There was no changing her mind when she was like that. She looked back at me.

"You've got to be grown-up about this, Melody," she said. "The estate agent called me when I was driving home and we've got our first viewing this evening."

"This evening?" I yelled.

"Yes," said Mum. She looked really tired. "I'm going to get changed."

She headed upstairs and I stood there for a

moment, trying not to cry.

"Come on, Frankie," I said. "Let's go for a walk."

I put my shoes on and clipped Frankie's lead on to his collar. As I closed the door I saw the FOR SALE sign again. The realization that this wasn't a big mistake smacked me right in the chest. Mum had denied it, but she'd clearly lied to me. So much for Team MC. We weren't a team in the slightest!

I hurried down the alleyway and into the graveyard. I was walking so fast that Frankie was struggling to keep up so I picked him up and tucked him under my arm. I went past the horse chestnut tree and the water tap and headed to the overgrown area with the crumbling wall.

I slowed down as I stumbled through the weeds. A stinging nettle brushed against my knee and that was when my tears began to fall. I climbed over the pile of bricks and stopped. The plague house stood still and silent in front of me. Now that I knew what it was, it looked spookier than ever. I wiped my cheeks with the back of my hand and walked up to the door.

I reread the sign across the doorframe and shivered. *Lord, Have Mercy Upon Us.* I checked for a painted cross on the door but there wasn't anything there. The door had probably been changed many times since the days of the plague.

It was still open and I squeezed through the small gap and into the first room. My eyes adjusted to the dim light and I put Frankie down on the ground. I listened for any creaking noises coming from upstairs, but all I could hear was the buzz of a bee going past the window and the caw of a distant crow.

I took a few, deep breaths and wiped the rest of my tears away. I looked around the room. There was a big crack running down one of the walls. It was so deep I could fit the tips of my fingers into the gap.

I walked through to the back room. It was a bit lighter today and a yellow sunbeam stretched across the room through the low window. Tiny specks of dust danced in the shaft of light. I looked around me, imagining the poor plague victims, all huddled together. I was glad Frankie was with me. I let go of his lead and he wandered around the room. He went to a corner and I could hear him snuffling and sniffing. He'd found something.

"What is it, Frankie?" I said.

I went over and saw it was a crumpled blanket.

I hadn't noticed it yesterday but the corners of the room were so dark it would have been easy to miss.

I looked for the pebble on the windowsill. It had gone.

"That's weird," I said. I looked around on the floor to see if it had fallen off, but there wasn't anything there.

I sat down on the thick stone window ledge and lifted Frankie up beside me. We looked through to the graveyard. I could see someone walking along the pathway in the distance, carrying a watering can as they tended a grave.

I sighed as I sat looking out of the window. The thought of leaving Chestnut Close made me feel physically sick. That house was all I'd ever known. I'd lived there since I was a baby. I'd learnt to ride a bike on the lawn in the back garden. Mum had brought Frankie into the house as a little pup; he'd scampered down the hallway and jumped into my lap and licked my face as I sat cross-legged on the kitchen floor. I remembered one time, when Dad had thrown a sheet over the dining room table, making me my own little den. He'd filled it with cushions and books and fairy lights and I'd spent a whole weekend under there.

Number three Chestnut Close was everything to me. It was my home.

When I thought of Dad, there was a part of me that wished, for a moment, that he was back with us. If Dad was still around then none of this would be happening. We'd have enough money and we wouldn't have to move at all. But then I remembered his lies and my stomach twisted into a giant knot once more.

CHAPTER 5

The last time I'd seen Dad was a few years back. Mum had bought tickets for the three of us to go to the circus, and I'd been looking forward to it for weeks. I'd never been to a circus before and I got more and more excited each time we drove past the giant red and white tent, pitched on a playing field in town. But, about an hour before we were due to leave, Mum said she had a really bad headache and wouldn't be coming.

"You go and enjoy your evening with your dad," she said. "He's away so much it'll be nice for you to spend a bit of time together." She smiled but her eyes looked a bit watery.

She was right about Dad being away a lot. He travelled with his job and sometimes was away for three or four weeks at a time. It was when he came home that the arguing would start. That was when I headed to the graveyard. Mum told me that they were just getting used to each other again and that spending time apart was tough for any relationship. It made sense so I didn't worry. It was just how my parents were.

In the car on the way to the circus we chatted about what kind of things we might see: from juggling clowns to tumblers and trapeze artists. Bright posters advertising the circus had been tied to lampposts in the high street for weeks. In the corner of the poster was a photograph of a tall black man who stared directly into the camera. He had handcuffs around his wrists and his ankles with a heavy-looking chain connecting the two. Behind him was a glass tank filled with water. Underneath the photo it read:

Featuring Our Special Guest
Underwater Escapologist Nicholas de Frey!

This was the act I was most excited about. How

could anyone escape from handcuffs while being underwater? It sounded impossible and terrifying!

When we got to the circus, Dad bought me a big bucket of caramel popcorn and a deluxe chocolate milkshake. He was never usually this generous, choosing the biggest and most expensive drink on the menu, but I wasn't going to complain.

"When is the esca– esca– escapologist going to be on?" I asked Dad as we sat in our seats. I was younger then and escapologist was a very long word.

"Not sure, maybe towards the end," said Dad. He was distracted by text messages that kept popping up on his phone. I nibbled at my popcorn and watched the seats around us begin to fill. It wasn't long before a woman's voice came over the speakers telling us that tonight's performance was about to begin and all mobile phones should be turned off. Dad switched his to silent and slipped it into his pocket.

The lights dimmed and the audience hushed. A woman in a red and black suit with shiny brass buttons appeared under the spotlight and welcomed all the families to the show, promising us a night we'd never forget. I squeezed Dad's hand

and he smiled at me.

The entertainment began with three jugglers throwing skittles to each other. Their tricks became more and more complex until they ended up juggling sticks of fire. It was incredible! Then there were acrobats and clowns and people in sparkling leotards spinning around on giant hoops. There were trapeze artists who somersaulted through the air, high up towards the billowing ceiling. It was so enthralling I kept forgetting to eat my popcorn and by the interval I hadn't even got through half of it.

"Do you think he'll be on after the break?" I asked Dad, who was checking his phone again.

"Who?" he said, typing something quickly on to his phone.

"Nicholas de Frey! The escapologist!" I said.

Dad turned to me at last.

"I expect so, Melody," he said. "Are you having a nice time?"

"It's the best thing I've ever seen!" I said. Dad smiled. I hoped he was enjoying it as much as me, even if he was distracted by his phone.

The second half was even better than the first. There was a sword swallower and a man who threw daggers at a woman who was spinning on a circular board. A few people in front of me couldn't bear to look and put their hands over their eyes, but I didn't want to blink.

The show went on and on and I started to worry that maybe Nicholas de Frey wouldn't be performing after all. Maybe something had gone wrong during rehearsals? Maybe he'd not been able to get out of the tank in time and there'd been a terrible accident? The thought made me feel a bit light-headed. But then the lights dimmed and a deep voice boomed over the speakers.

"Ladies and gentlemen, girls and boys ... please put your hands together and welcome our very special guest ... Nicholas de Frey and his assistant Amélie!"

The audience cheered and I clapped so hard I spilled quite a lot of popcorn. The lights were still low but I could make out a tall man and a shorter woman walking into the ring. They were followed by four other people dressed in grey, wheeling a box. When the lights went up I saw that it was a large, glass tank filled with water. It had a lid made of metal with a shackle and a padlock.

Nicholas de Frey was barefoot and wearing a white vest with dark trousers. He stood in front of the tank and raised both of his arms and everyone cheered. Beside him was a small, athletic-looking woman wearing a black vest with white trousers. She was Nicholas's assistant, Amélie. They both took hold of the large tank and circled it round to show us that there were no trapdoors or trickery hidden behind or underneath it. The water swirled and slopped against the sides as it moved.

Nicholas then held out his arms and Amélie produced some silver handcuffs from a black bag which she snapped on to his wrists. He walked around, holding his hands up above his head to show us how strong and sturdy the shackles were. He stood beside the tank and Amélie put some metal cuffs on to his ankles. She then threaded a large silver chain around the back of handcuffs and through the ankle cuffs, securing it with a heavy padlock. His hands and feet were now tied together – just like they had been on the poster.

I edged forward on to my seat. There was no way he was going to get out of that. Especially underwater! What if he couldn't hold his breath for long enough? Two men ran into the ring and stood either side of the tank, lifting off the heavy lid. They helped Nicholas into the water which reached up to his chest. He took a few, steady breaths. He was getting ready. Then he took one huge gulp of air and sank down so that he was completely underwater.

Things began to speed up. First, the two men slammed the heavy lid down and secured it with a large padlock. Amélie walked around the tank as Nicholas writhed around in the water. He pressed his hands against the glass and his eyes looked wide and frightened. The air in my lungs was already bursting and I let it out with a big huff.

"Is he going to be all right, Dad?" I panted. "He looks like he's in trouble!"

"Of course he's going to be OK," said Dad. "It's all part of the act."

The two men each held a long pole that was attached to a wide, black curtain. They circled the tank, hiding Nicholas from view. We couldn't see anything that was going on! I imagined Nicholas struggling in the water, his lungs bursting as he desperately tried to release his hands and feet from the shackles. The curtain shivered and trembled. I didn't want to blink in case I missed something and then, swoosh – the two men dropped the curtain to the ground. There was a huge gasp from the crowd as we stared at the tank of water.

It was empty! Nicholas had completely vanished! The chain, cuffs and the heavy padlock lay at the bottom of the tank of water.

The audience went crazy and people all around us got to their feet, cheering and yelling. I put my popcorn under my seat and stood up as well, clapping as loudly as I could. Amélie gave a deep bow, then skipped off out of the arena and behind a red curtain.

"That was incredible!" I said to Dad. "Did you see that? Where did he go?! That was amazing!" But Dad wasn't listening to me. He had his phone out again and was staring at it.

"More! Encore! More!" I shouted, copying the cries of the audience around me. My hands were sore from pounding them together. That was the best thing I had seen in my *whole life*!

But then Dad stood up too. He put his hand on my arm to stop me clapping and said that we had to go. Right now. As we pushed our way through the row of cheering people I realized I'd left my bucket of popcorn behind. I turned to go back, but Dad said to just leave it. We went out through the exit and back to the car. I guessed he just wanted to leave before everybody else did and beat the rush of traffic.

When we got home I told Mum that it had been the best night ever. She smiled at me, but her eyes looked a bit red. I asked her if she'd been crying and she just shook her head.

"I'm glad you had a good time, Melody," she said. She gave me a kiss and told me to get myself up to bed.

Dad gave me a big hug and kissed me on the top of my head.

"I love you, Melody," he said. He squeezed me tightly and I laughed as I wrestled myself free. I was so happy after such a brilliant evening.

The next day, everything changed.

I went downstairs to find Mum in the kitchen. She was sitting at the table, still wearing the clothes she had on last night. It looked like she hadn't been to bed at all. There was an open envelope in front of her and something scrunched up on the floor.

"Mum?" I said. "What's wrong? What's happened?"

"I'm sorry, Melody," said Mum, looking up at me. "Dad's gone. He's left us and he's never coming back."

"What?!" I said. "But . . . but he can't have!"

I ran to the lounge window. Dad's car was

missing from the driveway. I ran upstairs and opened his wardrobe but it was empty, apart from a few hangers. I went to the bathroom next. Surely Mum was wrong? He couldn't have just left? But in the bathroom were just two toothbrushes in our white, ceramic pot.

I went to my room and sat on my bed. My legs began to tremble.

I couldn't believe it.

Just like Nicholas de Frey, Dad had vanished.

CHAPTER 6

Frankie rested his head on my legs and I gently stroked the back of his neck as I sat in the window of the plague house. I'd been gone for a while now and, although I was angry with Mum, I didn't want her to worry. Worrying was the worst feeling in the world.

I put Frankie on the floor and picked up his lead and that was when I heard it again: the low, creaking noise coming from upstairs. I went into the first room.

"Hello?" I called. My heart was pounding. "Is somebody up there? You're not frightening me, you know. I'm not scared!"

Frankie cocked his head to one side and began to whine. I listened for a moment, but all was silent.

"Come on, Frankie," I said. "It was probably just the wind again."

We headed out and made our way over the broken wall and through the weeds. When I reached the main path, my foot rested on top of a memorial card. These little rectangular pieces of card were left by friends and family with flowers at funerals. I picked up the piece of card and when I walked past the litter bin I dropped it inside.

When we got to the end of the alleyway on to Chestnut Close I stopped and looked at the FOR SALE sign, casting a long, dark shadow across our driveway. There was a small, white car parked in the road outside our house. The viewers must still be there.

Hannah Jenkins was just coming out of number seven, manoeuvring a pram over the front step. She was wearing pink pumps, white jeans and a pale, lemon shirt. She looked a bit like an ice cream.

"Hello, Melody!" she called. "You haven't seen Rory, I mean Mr Jenkins, at all have you?"

Mr Jenkins taught sports at our school and was the meanest teacher there was. He particularly liked making Jake's life as miserable as possible.

"I think he runs the after-school athletics club today," I said.

"Oh yes. Silly me. Of course he does," she said. She was smiling but her sparkly white teeth were gritted together. She peered into the pram. "It looks like it's just the two of us going to Artful Crafters, doesn't it, Max?"

A little pink fist waved into the air. Artful Crafters was a place where you could go and paint a piece of pottery. They fired it for you and you went back on another day to pick it up. I'd been to a birthday party there once when I was at primary school. Most of the party had chosen unicorns and butterflies to paint but I'd chosen a snake.

"Isn't Max a bit young for painting?" I said.

Hannah laughed. "We're not painting anything – we're going to get our handprints put on a plate. A family keepsake of the three of us. I guess we'll just have to leave a space for Daddy's, won't we, Max?"

Wilson began barking from the kitchen. Through the front door I could see him throwing himself at a child gate. There was a tiny red ribbon tied into his fur on the top of his head. Frankie watched him and wagged his tail. Hannah sighed.

"I didn't even *want* a dog," she said. "Don't I have enough to do with a baby? What *was* Rory thinking?" I think she'd forgotten for a moment that I was there. She closed her front door and by the time she had turned back to me, her brilliant smile had reappeared.

"I see you're moving, Melody," she said, nodding to the FOR SALE sign. "That was a bit of a surprise. Are you going far?"

I crossed my arms. "No. There's been a mistake," I said. "Mum is ringing the estate agent right now."

Hannah's eyes darted to the white car, then back to me.

"I thought you had viewers?" she said.

I shook my head.

"I see. Anyway. It was nice to see you, Melody," Hannah said. I moved out of the way as she pushed the pram down the path and along the road towards town.

When I went in I could hear Mum in the dining room.

"And this is a lovely room in the summer months. It's south facing so we get the sun all day long." She came back through the kitchen and two men followed behind her.

"Hello, Melody!" she said. "I wasn't expecting you back so soon. This is Darren and Clive. They've come to look at the house!" Her voice was unnaturally high and she was grinning so hard it looked painful. I unclipped Frankie's lead and he trotted over to the two men to say hello.

"What do you think then?" I said. "Of the house?" One of the men bent down to stroke Frankie.

"It's ticking a lot of boxes. It's a lovely quiet road, isn't it, Darren? That's just what we're after."

Darren nodded. "We love the garden too. It's got a huge amount of potential. It's like a blank canvas."

I snorted. "Yeah, apart from when it floods in the winter. It's like a swamp out there for six months of the year, isn't it, Mum?"

Mum stared at me. "What are you talking about?" she said.

"And the road might seem quiet now but you wait until the weekend. Some of the neighbours like nothing more than throwing open their windows and playing their music. Especially number eleven," I said. "Mr Charles loves a bit of rock and roll. Do you like rock and roll music, Clive? Darren?"

Clive scrunched his nose up. "No. Not really," he said.

"Melody!" said Mum. She turned to them. "Melody is just trying to be funny. That's not true at all. It's a very quiet road."

"It wasn't quiet last summer," I said, ignoring Mum. "The whole street was swarming with police due to a kidnapping. You might have heard about it on the news? It was in *all* of the papers. *And* on TV."

Darren's Adam's apple bobbed up and down as he swallowed.

"A kidnapping?" he said. He turned to Mum. "Is that true?"

We all looked at Mum.

"Well, yes. That did happen," she said. "There was an incident involving a neighbour's grandchild but it's all resolved now."

Clive looked at his watch. "Right, well. Thank you for showing us around, Claudia. We've got a few more properties to view and..."

They edged towards the front door, saying their goodbyes very quickly. When the door closed behind them, Mum turned to me. I waited for her to get angry, to shout at me for ruining the viewing and for not being "mature" about everything. But she just looked really tired.

"I'm going for a bath," she said.

She slowly made her way upstairs. I went into the lounge and got my phone out of my school bag to text Matthew. He used to think mobile phones were deadly with germs hiding in the tiny crevices. But one day, not long after he started seeing Dr Rhodes, I got a text saying:

Guess who's got a phone?! Matthew

I really needed Matthew right now. I felt let down by Mum and I wanted to talk to my best friend. I wrote him a message:

Hi, Matthew. It's true. Mum has put our house up for sale. She wants us to move! I'm so worried. M x

I saw that the text had been read. I sat down on the sofa and stared at the screen, waiting for him to reply. I was sure that Matthew would have an idea about what I could do about this. He was really clever like that. While I was waiting I looked up all about plague houses and read a couple of articles.

Similar buildings were used to quarantine the sick in other countries too, and in Canada they were known as "fever sheds". It was all really fascinating.

Twenty minutes later and there was still no message from Matthew. I decided to put my phone down so I would stop staring at it. I went to the kitchen to get some fruit and a drink. Then I gave Frankie a brush and filled his water bowl. I waited until I heard Mum pull the plug out of the bath and then I went back into the lounge to check my phone.

There was no reply.

CHAPTER 7

I laid awake for hours worrying about moving house. Would I have to change schools? What about making new friends? The thought of going somewhere that I didn't know anyone made me feel ill.

When I got up the next morning, Mum went to give me a hug but I turned away.

"Melody, there's no need for that," she said. She looked hurt.

"There was no need for you to put the house up for sale without telling me, was there?" I snapped back. She sighed and picked up her bag.

"I'll see you later," she said. The front door

shut behind her. Her friend Erica had opened the organic café in town last year and they took it in turns to open up early, ready for the breakfast rush.

Matthew still hadn't answered my text but I decided that maybe he'd been having a bad evening and couldn't face using his mobile. At 7.55 a.m. I waited in our hallway looking through the small diamond window in our front door. The door of number nine opened and Matthew emerged, blinking into the daylight. I went out and quickly skipped across the close to join him.

"Hi, Matthew! Did you get my text?" I said. He frowned at me.

"Oh yeah. Sorry. I forgot to reply," he said.

I felt the smile melt from my face. He'd forgotten?

"Yeah, that's bad about you moving," he said, as we started walking along the road. "Really bad." I waited for him to say something else: something reassuring which would make me feel a little less worried, a little less alone. But he didn't. He didn't say *anything*! We walked in silence for a while.

"I went to the house in the graveyard again last night," I said. "I read up about plague houses afterwards. Did you know that the last major outbreak of the plague was in 1666? Plague houses were also called *pest houses* and *fever sheds*. They were used for other contagious diseases too, like typhoid or smallpox. We're vaccinated against those kinds of illnesses now though."

"Great," said Matthew. He didn't sound impressed. In fact, he didn't sound like he was really listening. Maybe he had germs on his mind again.

"How are you getting on with Dr Rhodes?" I asked. I knew he didn't like talking about it too much but I thought it was important to show that I cared.

"It's OK," said Matthew. "Some weeks are easier than others. One minute you don't feel too bad and the next you're terrified that the door handle you touched in the school corridor is contaminated with some deadly bacteria. That thought gets stuck in your mind and you think about it *constantly*. That's how OCD works."

That's what Matthew's condition was called. It stood for Obsessive Compulsive Disorder. I'd never heard of it before I knew Matthew.

"Dr Rhodes said it can take a while to unlearn all the things your brain has spent so long thinking are real," he said.

I nodded. That made sense.

It was nice, just the two of us, chatting. It had been so long since we'd spent any time together.

"If you ever want to talk, you know I'm a good listener," I said. Matthew smiled at me. I waited for him to say the same to me, especially now that our house was up for sale, but Jake was up ahead on his bike. I groaned. It looked like he was waiting for us.

"All right?" he said.

Matthew grinned at him. "All right?" he said back.

"Hey, Melody. Are you moving house?" Jake said.

I shook my head. "Nope," I said.

Jake jumped off his bike and walked beside us. "What do you mean, no? Your house is up for sale, isn't it?" he said.

I shrugged. "Mum won't go through with it," I said. "She knows how much I don't want to move."

Jake snorted. "Yeah, right." He seemed to find it all amusing. "I saw you going off to the graveyard again yesterday. You could move in there!" he said.

Jake laughed and I noticed that Matthew was grinning as if he found it funny too. My stomach churned. Why was Matthew being like this?

A voice hollered towards us from the school gates. "JAKE BISHOP!" It was Mr Jenkins. He was wearing black sweatpants and a tight black T-shirt. His arms were folded across his chest. He must be on morning gate duty this week. The three of us walked towards him.

"Do my eyes deceive me or are you actually on time for once, Bishop?"

Jake kept his head down. "Yes, Sir," he said, quietly.

"If you keep this up then you never know, you might be able to join the cross-country team. We meet at 7.30 a.m. on Wednesdays," Mr Jenkins said. "How about it?"

Jake blushed and didn't look up.

"Um. I can't ... um," said Jake.

"Oh yes. Of course," said Mr Jenkins. "You're not able to do anything that takes any *physical effort*, are you?"

I looked at Jake but he didn't say anything. "Jake can't do anything that means he'll get too hot and sweaty, Mr Jenkins. His skin reacts badly," I said. Mr Jenkins stared at me. I carried on. "He's got allergies and severe eczema. It's on his school records. Isn't it, Jake?" I looked at him but he was just staring down at the ground.

"Oh yes," said Mr Jenkins. "The mysterious 'skin condition'." He said it like he didn't really think such a thing existed. Then a group of Year Tens started pushing each other around and he rushed off to deal with them. We carried on through the gates.

"What did you say that for?" Jake said to me.

"About your skin? But it's true," I said. "Mr Jenkins knows you've got a valid reason. He's always picking on you. You should tell someone what he's like."

Matthew fidgeted nervously. Jake's face went red. "Like anyone is going to believe Jake Bishop!" He glared at me. "You've made everything worse! I'll just be more of a target next time. Keep your mouth shut, Melody Bird."

I looked at Matthew, waiting for him to defend me. We *were* friends after all. At last he opened his mouth. "Jake's right," said Matthew. "It's best to keep out of it, Melody."

My jaw dropped as Jake gave me a "told you so" look and then they both headed towards the playground.

CHAPTER 8

When I got back from school, Mum was in the lounge vacuuming.

"What are you doing home?" I said.

"Oh, hello to you too, Melody," she said, turning the vacuum off. "We've got another viewing in ten minutes so I left early to do a quick tidy round."

"Have you tried to get in touch with Dad?" I said, coldly. I didn't know if Mum even had his number any more and I'm pretty sure she changed her mobile number after he left. A few weeks after he left he began sending letters but she just ripped them up without reading them.

"Melody, we've been through this. We don't need

his help." She switched the vacuum back on and turned away.

"Well, we clearly do if we have to move house!" I yelled over the noise. Mum didn't look up. I went out to the hallway and got Frankie's lead. He was already sitting by the door waiting for me.

We walked down the alleyway and Frankie stopped to sniff at the usual clump of weeds. Sometimes I wondered if dogs left each other messages in their smells. I was just wondering what sort of message Frankie would leave when a voice made me jump.

"Off to hang out with the dead again, are you?" It was Jake, crouched down behind his garden wall. His bike was upturned and he had a spanner in his hand. His face looked red and sore in the sun.

"Why don't you try taking a day off being an idiot, eh Jake?" I said.

Jake laughed. "I'm only joking, Melody. You're so touchy. No wonder Matthew gets fed up with you."

I swallowed.

"What did you say?" I said.

He shrugged.

"Ah, nothing," he said. "It's just something he said when we went to the cinema the other night.

Something about you being ... how did he put it again? Oh yeah ... *exhausting*."

I opened my mouth to say something but nothing came out. Had Matthew *really* said that? I felt tears prickle my eyes. A door banged shut and we both looked up. Mr Jenkins emerged from number seven in shorts and a T-shirt. Wilson the puppy was wearing a red harness and yapping in circles at his feet.

"See you later," said Jake, and he hurried inside. He might act tough but that all changed when Rory Jenkins was around.

I watched as Mr Jenkins headed down the road, Wilson bouncing and criss-crossing in front of him.

I carried on along the alleyway and thought about what Jake had said. Was I really *exhausting*? It hurt to think that Matthew had said that about me. Didn't he want to be my friend any longer?

I took our usual loop around the graveyard so that Frankie could have a nice walk before we headed to the plague house. He trotted along, stopping to sniff at the occasional headstone. Someone had left a watering can beside the tap and Frankie gave that a good sniff too. I guessed that whoever had forgotten it would remember and come back for it soon.

The sky was heavy and grey and, even though it was spring, there was still a winter chill in the air. If it rained, I could just stay at the plague house until it stopped. In fact, I hoped it rained for hours, so I could shelter and not go home for as long as possible.

When we finished the loop, I began to walk towards the old, tumbling wall. Frankie was slowing down and I picked him up and carried him over the fallen bricks. I put him down on the grass and looked at the old building. It looked gloomier than ever. I felt a few spots of rain on my cheeks and then, all of sudden, it was like a giant tap had been turned on right above us.

"Come on, Frankie," I said. "Run!"

We reached the door and squeezed through the gap. I brushed the rain from my school skirt and the sleeves of my blazer. Frankie shook himself and wagged his tail.

"Are you all right?" I asked him. "That was wet." I looked around the room. "The next time we come here I might bring something to sit on. A couple of cushions or something," I said. I smiled to myself.

I could make it just like the den that Dad had made for me under the dining room table, only much bigger. I had some battery-powered fairy lights somewhere. I could bring some candles. A rug from my room, maybe. That would make the place feel less ... gloomy.

Just then, Frankie began to growl. He was staring towards the other room. A line of fur stood up along his back from his neck to his tail. His lips sneered, revealing the top row of his little pointed teeth.

"What's the matter, Frankie?" I said, looking towards the doorway. "What has spooked you?" The growls rumbled deep down in his throat and then he barked. I jumped.

"Frankie! That's enough!" I said, but he took no notice. The sharp barks bounced off the solid, brick walls and echoed around the room. I crouched down and put my hand on to his shoulder. I could feel him trembling as he began to growl again. He pulled towards the doorway but I held on to his collar.

"What is it, Frankie? What have you seen?" I said. I tried to laugh to make myself feel less frightened. "Is it a big, scary mouse? Or a hairy spider? Or maybe you've seen a ghost and..."

I stopped. A shadow moved across the floor in the other room. I stood up, my heart pounding, and took a few steps to the doorway. That's when I saw something else. There was a rucksack in the corner, next to the dirty blanket. It definitely hadn't been there yesterday. And the small, round pebble was back on the window ledge.

"Hello?" I said. "Is there someone here?"

Silence.

"I warn you," I said. "I've got a fierce dog with me!"

I looked down at Frankie, who had stopped growling and was busy licking his bum.

I walked further into the room and went over to the rucksack. It was unzipped and I peered inside.

"Stop! That's private property!" said a voice.

I jumped and spun round. At first, I couldn't tell where the voice was coming from, it was so dark. But then someone stepped out from behind the door.

It was a boy. He looked to be a few years older than me and a couple of inches taller. He was wearing a red knitted cardigan, a grey T-shirt and a pair of jeans that were much too short for him. His face was so pale it looked translucent. Like a ghost, or someone with the plague.

"Are ... are you ... one of them?" I croaked.

The boy frowned. His arms hung awkwardly down by his sides as if he didn't know what to do with them.

"One of who?" he said.

I swallowed. "A ... plague victim," I said.

The boy shook his head. "No," he said.

His eyes flittered around the room and I noticed he was breathing quickly. He seemed just as nervous as I was. Frankie pulled me towards the boy, his paws slipping on the wooden floor and his tail wagging madly. So much for my fierce dog. I edged closer and watched as the boy knelt down and patted Frankie's head. He was stroking him like a two-year-old might.

"He's so soft," he said, looking up at me.

"He's called Frankie," I said. "Like a frankfurter."

The boy looked blank.

"A frankfurter sausage?" I continued. "You know how dachshunds are sometimes called sausage dogs? That's how we came up with his name."

The boy didn't say anything. Frankie rolled on to his back and the boy gently tickled his tummy.

"Anyway, who are you and what are you doing

here?" I said. I was angry that my secret house was being shared by someone who I didn't even know. The boy didn't say anything for a moment. He seemed to be trying to work out what to say.

"I could say the same to you," he said at last, standing up. "Who are *you* and what are *you* doing here?"

I lifted my chin. "I'm Melody," I said. "Melody Bird."

"Melody Bird," he said, thoughtfully. "That's an interesting surname – Bird. Did you know that a flock of crows is called a murder?"

I stared at him and shook my head. "Who are you?" I asked again.

The boy just stared back at me. I didn't like him talking about murder, or that he wouldn't tell me who he was. There was a low, distant rumble of thunder that sounded a bit like one of Frankie's growls. I wasn't sure I wanted to be there any longer.

"Right. Well, anyway. We'd better be going now," I said. I headed to the door but the boy stepped forward to block our way.

"You won't tell anyone I'm here, will you?" he said.

"I might," I said. "You won't tell me your

name and you're acting all suspicious. You could be anyone."

The boy thought about it for a moment and then his face lit up. "Hey, do you like magic tricks?" he said.

I frowned. He ran to the windowsill and picked up the small, grey pebble. He pushed his sleeves halfway up his arms then took the pebble, and placed it in the centre of his right palm. He turned his left hand over and back again to show it was empty. Then he swapped the pebble to the left and then turned his right hand over and back again. Then he opened both hands. The pebble had vanished!

"That's amazing!" I said.

He smiled then walked towards me. I took a step back as he reached a hand towards my left ear. He took his hand away and opened his fist. In the centre of his palm was the grey pebble.

I laughed. "You can do magic!" I said.

He grinned at me. "I can," he said. I frowned at him again. I knew exactly what he was trying to do. He was trying to distract me. Magicians were good at that.

"So, now will you tell me who you are?" I

said. His face dropped and he walked over to the windowsill, placing the grey pebble back.

"I can't," he said, bluntly.

"Why not?" I said.

He stared down at Frankie who had settled on his tummy with his head between his front paws.

"Um. It's... it's... none of your business," he said.

I sighed. "OK. Whatever," I said. "Come on, Frankie. We need to get home."

The boy looked up.

"Hang on. You've got to swear you won't tell anyone before you go. It's really important," he said. His blue eyes were wide open and I noticed how thin he looked underneath the red cardigan. I could see the outline of his ribs against his T-shirt. I just shrugged and headed back to the other room.

"Wait, Melody Bird!" he shouted.

I slowly turned around and stared at the pale, thin boy in the red knitted cardigan. "I'll tell you why I'm here, but you must promise not to tell a living soul."

"You want me to promise?" I said.

He nodded.

"That depends. I don't want to promise if it turns out you've just killed someone or that you're a criminal or something. I'd have to tell *someone* then," I said.

He seemed to think about it for a moment. "I'm neither of those," he said.

I pretended to think about it but I already knew my answer. "OK. I promise," I said.

I watched as he chewed on his lip. He still didn't say anything.

"Well, go on then," I said. "Who are you?"

He stared at the ground and I thought he might have decided not to tell me after all. Or maybe he was searching to find the right words. But then he looked up and his bright, blue eyes met mine.

"My name is Hal Vincent," he said. "And I am a spy."

CHAPTER 9

My first thought was that I didn't think spies wore red knitted cardigans. Spies wore inconspicuous clothes like dark suits or long, grey mackintosh coats. Clothes that would help them to blend into the background. This boy was wearing trousers that were far too short for him and a cardigan that could be seen from about three miles away. He stood a little taller in front of me.

"A spy?" I said. Hal nodded. Frankie sat back down, realizing we weren't leaving after all. I wound his lead a couple of times around my hand.

"You don't look like a spy," I said, cautiously. "You look too ... ordinary."

Hal smiled. "That's deliberate, of course. Who would suspect me?"

"You don't look old enough to be a spy, either," I said. "How old are you? Fifteen? Sixteen at the most?"

"I'm old enough," he said. "And anyway. Who says that spies have to be adults? We have to look like the people that you would least expect."

I still wasn't convinced. "That doesn't sound right," I said.

"Let me put it this way," he said. "There is a lot of highly confidential work happening around all of us, Melody Bird. Even *I* don't know about all of it. But what I *do* know is that sometimes, us not knowing is in our best interest. Do you understand?"

I thought for a moment. "No, not really," I said. "Anyway, there can't be much spy-work in a graveyard."

"That's where you're wrong," he said. "Follow me." He turned back into the other room. I stood there for a moment, wondering if I should just go home and leave this boy to his strange, make-believe world. I was intrigued, though. I followed, keeping Frankie close, and stood in the doorway.

Hal was standing by the dirty window. The corners were thick with spiders' webs and a collection of dead flies lay belly-up along the edge of the glass.

"There he is." Hal checked a digital watch on his wrist. "Right on time." He glanced at me.

"You can come and see if you like. But keep out of sight. He's *highly* dangerous."

I walked closer. All I could see was the crumbling wall, the tops of the weeds and some of the gravestones.

"There's no one there," I said, quietly.

"Look closer. He's over there, on the right," whispered Hal.

I took a few more steps until I was standing right beside him. This time I saw who he was pointing at. Through the gap in the wall and across the weeds I could see a man. He was standing in front of one of the newer headstones by the main path, sheltering under a red umbrella with his head slightly bowed.

"*That*," said Hal, "is Martin Stone. One of the most notorious criminals of the twenty-first century."

The man looked to be around sixty years old or so and he was wearing dark trousers and a light-beige jacket. He took a white handkerchief out of his pocket, shook it open with one hand, then blew his nose. He didn't look like a notorious criminal to me.

"Are you sure?" I said. "He looks ... well, ordinary."

Hal snorted. "Ha. Yes, he probably does. He likes to pretend that he's just a regular guy, but we've been tracking him for months."

I wondered who he meant by "we".

"What has he done?" I asked.

Hal smirked. "What *hasn't* he done," he said. "Martin Stone has left a path of devastation behind him. Grievous bodily harm, money laundering, blackmail, theft. That's the one we're hoping to get him on. We believe he was behind the theft of a valuable necklace, known as the 'Kingfisher Necklace', taken from the Fitzwilliam Museum in Cambridge in 2015. The precious jewels match the colours of the bird: an orange and a blue sapphire, an emerald and diamonds. Our sources lead us to believe that, at last, the necklace is on the move to a new home. Martin Stone might make the handover any day now."

I watched as the man stretched his palm out from beneath the umbrella. It wasn't raining any more and he closed the umbrella and gave it a shake. He took one more look at the grave and then turned away.

"He's going!" I said, watching as the top of the man's head disappeared from view. "Shouldn't you do something? Follow him?"

Hal shook his head.

"I'm not here to arrest him. I'm here to observe. To make notes. To report back to my officials. We need to find out where the Kingfisher Necklace is first. *Then* we can make a move. That necklace is the key to his arrest. If we can catch him in the act of dealing stolen goods, we've got him."

I looked outside as the rain dripped off the leaves of a tree. I wasn't sure about any of this.

Hal turned away slightly, pulled his sleeve back, and began to talk into the digital watch on his wrist. "The stone has moved. I repeat, the stone has moved. Over," he said.

I listened for a reply but didn't hear one. I tried to see if he was wearing an earpiece but his brown hair was quite long over his ears so I couldn't tell.

"Who were you talking to?" I said.

Hal looked up and I thought I saw a twinkle in his eyes.

"I'm guessing you've heard of MI5 and MI6?" he said. I nodded.

"Well my bosses are MI8. It's a tight team – the Warley Tower branch. We're small, but highly effective."

"Hang on a minute," I said. "You're called Hal Vincent and you're working for the Warley Tower branch of MI8. And you're staking out a dangerous criminal called Martin Stone, who is wanted for theft a few years back. I'm not being funny but ... are you supposed to be telling me any of this? Isn't it *classified*?" I folded my arms and raised my eyebrows.

Hal pressed the tips of his fingers together. "We only share the things we want you to know, Melody Bird," he said. "We are trained for encounters with members of the public and have the skills to use this contact to our advantage." He smiled. "Have you considered that maybe I'm deliberately sharing this information with you to help me with the case?"

I looked around the bleak, cold room and then towards the crumpled blanket and on the floor and the rucksack. On the blanket was a pencil case and a notepad.

"If you're a spy then I'm guessing you know what this place used to be?" I said.

Hal didn't react.

"It was a plague house," I said. "This was where they locked up the sick to keep them from infecting others. Can you imagine how terrifying that must have been? Trapped in a cold, dark building, knowing that you were just ... waiting to die."

Hal's eyes darted around the room.

"That's awful," he whispered.

I nodded. "Yep. They would have been writhing in agony, knowing that they'd never feel sunlight on their faces *ever again*," I said. I stayed silent. All you could hear was the wind rattling against the window pane.

Suddenly, Frankie shook himself, making his collar jingle and we both jumped.

"But, I guess this kind of thing isn't scary for a real-life *secret agent* is it?" I said.

Hal didn't say anything. His face had drained of any colour.

"Right, well, I'm going now," I said. "I can't *wait* to tell my mum about this."

Hal took a step towards me and gripped the tops of my arms.

"No, Melody Bird! You cannot tell a soul that I am here," he said. "You'll ruin all the work that I've done. If anyone knows I'm here then all of our work will have been for nothing. The entire operation would be blown. Martin Stone will walk away, just like he has all the other times."

I shook him off and took a step backwards. I recognized the look in his eyes; I'd seen it in Matthew's when he thought he'd come into contact with germs. He was scared. Hal definitely wasn't faking that part.

"It's imperative that no one knows I'm here. There are some *really* dangerous criminals out there," he said. His eyes turned to the window again. "My life could depend on it."

"That man didn't look *anything* like a criminal," I said.

"You have no idea what he is capable of," Hal said. "If Martin Stone or one of his gang find out I'm here ... then I'll be wishing I was just a plague victim!"

The look of fear in his eyes was making me nervous. Was that old man *really* dangerous? Could Hal be telling the truth? I needed time to think it over.

"OK," I said.

Hal gave me a small smile.

"I really do have to go, though," I said. "I live in Chestnut Close, just through the alleyway. I walk Frankie here every day so I might see you again. If you're still trying to catch criminals, of course."

Hal sniffed. "Maybe," he said. "But don't let anyone see you coming here."

I nodded and walked back to the front door with Frankie. We went outside and made our way through the damp weeds. There was definitely something very strange going on here. I just needed to figure out exactly what it was. I should talk to Mum and let her know what was going on. After all, I hadn't *actually* said the words "I promise" to Hal.

We walked down the alleyway and I stopped. Mum was standing on the doorstep, waving at someone getting into a car. They drove off down Chestnut Close. It must have been someone viewing the house. I stepped out of sight and waited until our front door closed.

Suddenly, any thoughts about telling Mum about Hal in the graveyard vanished. Mum had lied to me. She'd kept a secret *so big*. We had to leave our home and she hadn't even told me. Frankie looked up at me, wondering why we'd stopped. I made up my mind.

If Mum could keep a secret from me, then I could certainly keep one from her.

CHAPTER 10

The next day was Saturday. I hadn't set my alarm but I still woke up early.

I turned my phone on and searched on the internet for any mention of MI8. They had once existed, but during World War 2. I then searched "stolen kingfisher necklace" and found a newspaper report. It was real! A necklace *had* been stolen from a museum in Cambridge back in 2015. No one was ever prosecuted and the necklace was never found. The police believed it was unlikely that it would ever be recovered.

So one thing was true, at least. I decided I'd go back to the plague house and see if I could find out more.

I had a shower and got dressed, then went downstairs to get breakfast. As I was buttering my toast, Mum came into the kitchen through the back door. She was carrying some gloves, a saw, some clippers and a large green sack.

"Hello, love," she said. "I'm going to cut down that old tree in the front garden. Fancy giving me a hand?"

The front garden was mostly a driveway and a dead conifer tree which stood in one corner. Mum had never bothered with the garden much before the house was on the market.

All of this was a waste of time. I wasn't going anywhere.

"I can't," I said. "I'm going to the graveyard this morning."

"It won't take long," said Mum. "And it'll do you good to have a break from that place for a while. It's not healthy, Melody, being surrounded by all that death ... all that sadness."

It baffled me how anyone could find the graveyard a sad place. To me, it was full of history and beauty and, now, a boy who claimed to be a *spy*. I opened my mouth to say something about Hal but closed it again. She'd kept her secret and I could keep mine.

"*Please*, Melody," she said, waving a pair of gardening gloves at me. "Team MC?"

I sighed and finished my piece of toast. Hal and the graveyard would have to wait.

Cutting down the conifer was almost the first time Team MC had been defeated. The trunk was thick and Mum's small saw was too blunt to cut through it. We tried to dig around the base hoping that we'd be able to lift it up from the roots, but after an hour we still hadn't got anywhere. Frankie lay on the front door mat in the sun. Every now and then he lifted his head to check we were still there, then laid his head back down again.

"I'm going to see if I can borrow a better saw from Mr Charles," said Mum, wiping the sweat from her forehead. "I won't be long."

Mr Charles lived in the house next to Matthew's. He was always pottering around his garden so he was bound to have something we could use. While I waited I snipped at a few of the branches on the dead conifer.

Two front doors banged shut and Matthew and Jake both came down their paths at the same time.

They made their way over.

"Hi, Melody," said Matthew.

"Hi," I said. "Where are you two off to?"

"The high street," said Jake. "There's a new gaming place we want to take a look at, don't we?" He looked at Matthew, who nodded.

"Oh," I said. "I didn't think you were into gaming, Matthew?"

He shrugged. "I'm just having a look," he said.

Jake started laughing. "Yeah, well, it beats hanging around a graveyard, any day!" he said.

I pressed my lips together and glared at Jake. I almost told him about the plague house and how interesting things had become over there, but I stopped myself. I turned to Matthew.

"Why don't we go into town next weekend?" I said. "We could go to Mum's café and get a milkshake."

Jake snorted and Matthew shrugged.

"Um, I dunno," he said. "Maybe."

It was clear he wasn't keen. I kept my chin up and tried to look like I wasn't bothered.

"Come on, Matthew. Let's go," said Jake.

Matthew gave me a weak smile and they turned away and began to walk down Chestnut Close towards the high street. It was only then that I allowed the smile on my face to crumble.

It took Team MC another hour to cut the conifer down, even with the brand new garden saw that Mum had borrowed from Mr Charles. While we worked, he stood and watched us.

"If you angle the saw downwards a little more, Claudia, you'll find it will grip much better," he said.

Mum didn't reply.

"Not like that," said Mr Charles. "Tell you what, let me have a go."

"Thank you, Mr Charles," said Mum. Her voice muffled amongst the branches. "We're managing just fine."

"Are you sure?" said Mr Charles. "Because your technique is all wrong. I'm happy to . . ."

"WE'RE FINE. THANK YOU," Mum yelled through the branches.

"Oh. Right you are," said Mr Charles.

I'd never known Mum to ask anyone for help. After Dad left she said that the two of us could do anything if we put our mind to it – and we had.

Mr Charles took a silver key with a little red

plastic fob attached to it out of his trouser pocket. "If you don't need me then, Claudia, I'll just pop to number one and check the place over. I'll be back in a jiffy," he said.

"Thank you, Mr Charles. No need to rush," said Mum from deep within the conifer.

Mr Charles hesitated for a moment, then walked off. I took a breather and watched him go. He went up the driveway of the house next door and used the key to go inside.

Number one Chestnut Close had been empty for months now. Every couple of weeks or so Mr Charles checked that everything was OK, collected the post and made sure there were no leaky pipes or anything. The owners' children lived abroad with their families so they weren't around to do it themselves.

"At last!" said Mum as she managed to saw through the last bit of trunk. The crusty-brown conifer slumped on to the drive like it had suddenly fainted. Mum straightened up and wiped her forehead.

"Well done, Mum. You did it!" I said. For a moment I forgot I was angry with her and felt proud that she'd achieved what she'd set out to do.

That's what Team MC was all about: not giving up. I helped her drag the dead tree into the back of our car so that she could take it to the recycling centre.

"Thank you, Melody. I'm glad that's out of the way," she said, slamming the boot shut. "I won't be long." She climbed into the driver's seat and gave me a wave as she reversed off the drive.

I went inside and Frankie followed me, flopping into his bed in the kitchen. I'd take him out for his walk later. I grabbed an apple from the fruit bowl and my key from the hallway table, then shut the door. I trotted across our cul-de-sac and headed down the alleyway between the Rectory and Jake's house at number five. To the graveyard.

CHAPTER 11

It was a warm day and some of the long, pale grass looked golden in the sunlight. It was so beautiful there in the cemetery, even the overgrown bits. I ate my apple as I scrambled through the weeds, brambles and over the bricks to get to the plague house.

I squeezed through the front door and went inside. "Hal, are you here?" I called. I burst into the back room to see Hal uncurling from the blanket on the floor. He blinked at me, looking a bit dazed. His rucksack was still in the dusty corner.

"Hang on a minute. Are you *sleeping* here?" I said.

Hal sat up. He rubbed at his eyes, then pointed at my half-eaten apple.

"Do you want that?" he said.

I looked at the apple in my hand.

"Um. I guess not," I said. "Do you?"

He nodded, slowly. I handed the apple to him and he began eating it.

"Is everything ... OK?" I said. He shook his head.

"There's been a technical hitch," he said. Tiny pieces of white apple flesh fell out of the side of his mouth. "A malfunction in the Warley Tower branch communication."

"What do you mean, a malfunction?" I asked.

Hal concentrated on the apple for a moment. He was eating it right down to the pips.

"My communication device has failed," he said. He lifted his wrist. I remembered he'd spoken into his watch yesterday – apparently communicating with his team. To me it looked too old-fashioned to do anything other than tell the time.

"In a situation like this, the protocol is to just sit tight." He slowly stood up. "I think Martin Stone's gang might have something to do with it. They've probably blocked the signal. I've just got to be patient and wait for instructions."

"Instructions from MI8, is that right?" I said. He

nodded. "Well, that's interesting, because I looked them up and they haven't existed since the 1940s."

Hal smiled. "Melody Bird, MI8 is a *secret organisation*. We are not exactly going to be advertising what we do all over the internet now, are we?"

I looked at the thin blanket on the floor.

"And they've just left you here without any food? Or a bed?" I said.

"None of that is your concern, Melody Bird," Hal said. "I'm trained for this kind of eventuality. I've been in far worse situations than just sitting it out in a graveyard, I can tell you. And if I want to, I can disappear."

I raised my eyebrows.

"Really? How?" I said.

"As if by magic," Hal said, clicking his fingers and grinning. I thought about the pebble that had vanished right before my eyes and Nicholas de Frey disappearing from the tank of water. My tummy fizzled. I absolutely *loved* magic.

Hal crossed his arms and turned to stare out of the window. Was he thinking of disappearing right now? He had his back to me and I quickly closed my eyes and counted to three. When I opened them he was still there. I was being silly. People didn't just vanish into thin air! Apart from Dad. Although Dad hadn't used magic. He'd just lied.

"Hal. Are you really telling the truth about all of this?" I said. "Are you sure it's not made up?"

He turned around, frowning slightly. "I'm Special Agent Hal Vincent, MI8 Warley Tower branch," he said. "It's not a lie."

I studied his face.

"Someone lied to me once. And it really hurt," I said. "I think lying is one of the worst kinds of betrayals, don't you?"

"What happened?" said Hal. "Who lied to you?"

I walked over to the window. I'd never told anyone about what happened after the circus. Not even Matthew. The only people who knew about Dad's lies were me and Mum. Everyone else just thought Mum and Dad had agreed to separate.

"I don't want to talk about it," I said. "You just have to believe me when I say I refuse to be lied to, ever again."

Hal nodded. "Well, Melody Bird," he said. "I can tell you right here and now that Special Agent Hal Vincent is not a liar. OK?"

"OK," I replied. I still wasn't sure but I did feel

a bit happier hearing him say that. It was odd how he kept using my full name. Maybe that was how special agents spoke?

We stood there in silence for a bit and then Hal walked over and sat down on his blanket, crossing his ankles. A shadow fell across the lower half of his face.

"So, you must have quite an exciting life then," I said. "As a spy. My life is just so ... ordinary."

He grinned. "I don't think you're ordinary in the slightest," he said. "I don't expect there are many people who like hanging out in plague houses for a start. You sound pretty unique to me."

I smiled. I'd been called weirdo, strange and odd in the past, but never *unique*. I liked it!

"Tell me all about the world of Melody Bird," Hal said. "I bet it's more interesting than you realize."

He tucked his knees up under his chin and I went and sat on the corner of the blanket.

"Well, I've lived in Chestnut Close for my whole life, so that's thirteen years. Although Mum has got this ridiculous idea that we're moving," I said. "It's a cul-de-sac so it's like our own little private road, really. There's just the two of us. Oh, and Frankie of course."

"Of course," said Hal. "The little dog that looks like a furry sausage!"

I giggled.

"The house adjoining ours is empty, but on the other side of us there is this really brilliant, creepy house called The Rectory. That's where Old Nina lives."

"Old Nina?" said Hal. "How *old* is she?"

"It's just a nickname!" I said. "No one calls her that to her face. Actually, you can see the back of her garden and the house from the graveyard. It's only over there."

I pointed in the rough direction of The Rectory. "Next to her is number five where Jake Bishop lives with his mum, Sue. His older brother moved to Australia recently so it's just the two of them as well. Jake is in my year at school. He can be an idiot sometimes."

"How is he an idiot?" said Hal. I wondered how I could describe Jake to someone who had never met him before.

"He can just be a bit … nasty. I almost think he doesn't realize he's doing it. Matthew says it's because he was bullied because of his allergies when he was little. His skin looks red-raw sometimes and people used to pick on him and call him names. I don't think that's an excuse for being rude to other people though, do you?" I said. Hal shook his head.

"And who is Matthew?" he said. "Does he live next to Jake?"

"No. Next to Jake are the Jenkins at number seven. Hannah, Rory and a baby called Max. They've just got a new puppy called Wilson who yaps all the time. Rory Jenkins is our PE teacher at school and everybody hates him. Especially Jake. He picks on Jake a lot. Even when he doesn't deserve it."

Hal nodded. "That might also explain why Jake is nasty sometimes," he said, picking at a piece of fluff on his cardigan. I frowned. I wasn't sure why Mr Jenkins being horrible to Jake would make Jake want to be horrible to other people, but I carried on.

"Next to the Jenkins is number nine where Matthew lives with his mum, Sheila, and dad, Brian. Oh, and his cat, Nigel. Although Matthew doesn't really like animals as he thinks they carry germs. His parents are *lovely*. And Matthew is one of the strongest people I know. He's been through a lot *and* he solved a crime last year! A boy called Teddy Dawson went missing from the close.

Matthew worked out what had happened. He was a bit of hero for a while!"

Hal nodded thoughtfully. "I think I remember that happening. It was in the newspapers."

I smiled. I was proud of what Matthew had done.

"It sounds like Matthew means a lot to you," he said. I shrugged.

"I guess. He was my best friend, although I'm not so sure now. He's started hanging out with Jake more," I said. I was about to say that I didn't think he even liked me much any more, but my throat caught.

"He's better friends with 'idiot' Jake over you? He must be mad," said Hal. That made me feel a little better.

"And who lives next to Matthew?" said Hal.

"That's the last house in Chestnut Close," I said. "Number eleven where Mr Charles lives. He's retired and spends a lot of time in his front garden, chatting to anyone who comes past."

"He sounds very lonely," said Hal.

I screwed up my nose. "No, I don't think so. I just think he likes talking a lot."

Hal shrugged as if to say "maybe". I'd never thought of Mr Charles as lonely before.

"And, that's everybody! That's Chestnut Close," I said.

Small wrinkles appeared in the corner of Hal's eyes as he smiled to himself. I looked down at the apple core on the floor.

"Do you want me to get you something to eat?" I said. "You must be starving."

Hal rubbed his forehead. "I'm not sure about that," he said. "I don't want to put you at any risk."

"It wouldn't!" I said. "I'll be completely incognito."

He rested his chin on his knees. He seemed to be giving it some serious thought.

"Do you think you can do it without anyone, and I mean *anyone* knowing? You can't tell your mum or Matthew or Jake or that Old Nina woman or Mr Charles. *Nobody* can know I'm here."

I could feel goose bumps prickle down my arms. "Absolutely! No one will know, Hal. Your secret is safe with me. I promise." He took a few long breaths.

"I guess once won't do any harm," he said. "I've been using the tap in the graveyard for drinking water and the toilet in the church. Food is something I can't get. Would you be able to get me something that might keep me going me for a while? You know – fuel food. Fruit, nuts, that kind of thing?"

"No problem," I said. "Do you need anything else?"

"Um, maybe a change of clothes. And a torch. It gets quite dark here at night."

"OK," I said. My mind was racing as I tried to think where I'd get clothes from.

"A pair of binoculars would be good too," continued Hal.

I added them to my mental list. This was going to take some doing. Hal smiled at me.

"The Warley Tower branch will be indebted to you, Melody Bird," he said. "I'll make sure they know how important you've been to this mission."

I stood up and spotted something through the window.

"Look! He's back," I said. Hal got up and joined me. Martin Stone was standing by the grave again. He was wearing the same clothes that he had on yesterday – dark trousers and a beige jacket – but this time he wasn't carrying an umbrella. He bent down and fiddled with the rose bush, then lifted a watering can and poured some water on to the grave. Hal stood beside me and watched him.

"How are you going to report Martin Stone's movements if you can't contact your branch?" I said. "Isn't that the whole point of you being here?"

"I can make notes of times and dates to work out if there is a pattern. It's all vital information," Hal said.

The elderly man emptied the watering can and placed it down by his feet, then he took a mobile phone out of his jacket pocket and began to type something into the screen, slowly, using one finger.

"This is *so* frustrating," said Hal, slapping his hand against the wall. "He might be liaising with an associate. If I could communicate to our team we'd be able to intercept that message right now and it might lead us to the Kingfisher Necklace! The case could be cracked!"

Martin Stone put his phone away, picked up his watering can and turned to leave.

"It looks like he's going for the day," said Hal. "Something is definitely going on here. That necklace is probably closer than we realize. I'm convinced it's going to be moved soon."

I thought about all that he'd told me. MI8. Martin Stone. A stolen necklace. An unsolved theft. A stakeout. I still wasn't entirely convinced by his story. It still sounded a bit like a movie script, or a game.

"I'll go and get your things now," I said. "Unless you wanted to add anything else. A pen with a hidden camera, perhaps?"

Hal seemed to consider it. I don't think he even realized I was joking.

"No. Just the other things would be fine," he said. "And thank you again, Melody Bird. What you are doing is incredibly important and MI8 will be incredibly grateful. You'll be a part of the team, in a way."

My heart began to beat a little faster. Part of a real-life spy team. Was he for real?

"No problem," I said with a grin.

CHAPTER 12

I followed the route back through the trampled weeds and came out on to the main path.

I felt quite sorry for Hal – whether he was a spy or not. Sleeping in a cold, dark plague house on just a thin blanket must be horrible. I was pretty sure that Mum had a thick blanket in the bottom of her wardrobe that she wouldn't miss. I'd add that to the list of things. The food and torch would be easy to take, and I knew Matthew had some binoculars so I could see if I could borrow them. I couldn't ask him for any clothes though. That would make him ask too many questions.

As I walked I heard someone whistling a little

song. It was a man, standing by the water tap. I gasped. It was Martin Stone! He hadn't left the graveyard at all! He'd just gone to refill his watering can. My throat tightened and I froze. I thought about what Hal had said – that this man was the criminal brain behind one of the country's biggest jewellery thefts and *very* dangerous. Perhaps I should go back to the plague house and warn him? But then, if Martin spotted me, that might lead him to Hal.

I heard the slow creak of the tap and a shot of water as it blasted into the metal can. I carried on edging forward, watching him all the time. His shoulders were slightly stooped and he was wearing a pair of white trainers, probably for comfort rather than running. He really didn't look dangerous at all.

I could tell by the sound of the water that the can was nearly filled. He still had his back to me, and as he bent forward to turn off the tap, I saw there was something hidden beneath his jacket. It was made of brown leather and was tied around his waist like a thick belt. Resting against his hip and attached to the belt was a long pocket. I squinted, then gasped.

It was a gun! In a holster! I could even make out the grey handle poking out of the top! Hal *was* telling the truth! He *was* a secret agent, he *was* staking out a criminal, and he *did* work for MI8. There was a man with a gun, right here in the graveyard – it was real!

I felt a mix of terror but also excitement. I started walking again, quicker this time. As exciting as this was, I really didn't want to come face to face with an armed criminal. But then, as I snuck past, Martin Stone suddenly span around.

"Hello there!" he said.

I froze. My mouth hung open.

"I've got to do this or they'll die," Martin said, staring at me.

I swallowed. "Who will die?" I asked. It came out as a squeak.

"The roses. They were my wife's favourite," he said. "In this hot weather they need at least two cans of water a day, I'd say. Even after all that rain yesterday."

He bent down to pick up the can and as he did, I noticed he held his jacket closed. He was hiding the gun!

"Who are you here to see, then?" he said.

At first, I thought he was talking about Hal and my stomach did a somersault, but then I realized he meant who was I seeing out of the dead people.

"My Great Uncle ... erm ... Bob."

"That's lovely, a youngster like you showing your respect like that," said Martin, smiling. Some of the water splashed out of the can and on to his trousers but he didn't seem to notice.

"Where's your Great Uncle Bob then?" he said. "Got a nice plot, has he?"

I nodded. "Yes, he's over ... by the, erm..." My mind raced. If Martin found out there wasn't an Uncle Bob after all then I could be in serious trouble. And Hal too. "Actually, he hasn't got a plot," I said. "He's everywhere! His ashes were scattered under the, um, horse chestnut tree so I just come here sometimes and ... think about him."

Martin Stone stared at me, his forehead furrowed. He had a scar across one eyebrow which made it look like it had been sliced in two. I suspected it was from a fight. A fight with another gangster, perhaps! I shivered.

"Well, I must say I think that is just wonderful," he said. His face melted into a soft smile. "You enjoy your happy thoughts about your Great Uncle Bob. Cheerio now."

He slowly walked away, the water slopping out

of the can as he went. As soon as he was at a safe distance I sprinted along the pathway then straight down the alleyway towards home.

CHAPTER 13

I couldn't wait to tell Hal all about my encounter with Martin Stone, but first I had to get his supplies.

Mum was still out, so I had the house to myself. I found an old plastic bag in a drawer and shook it open. Frankie came sniffing around as I went through the cupboard. He needed a walk but I'd take him out later.

I thought about what Hal had said about suitable "fuel" food. It sounded like a sensible request and was probably all part of his spy-training. I settled on: a packet of crackers, a small box of raisins, two bananas, three nut bars and an orange. I sliced some cheese which he could put on to the crackers and put it into a little plastic tub.

I raked through the kitchen drawer that was full of old phone chargers, sticky tape and screws that we didn't have any use for. At the back I found a torch. I tested it and miraculously it still worked. There was also a pack of cards with pictures of farmyard animals on one side. I smiled. Maybe Hal could show me some more magic tricks. I threw everything into the carrier bag.

I went upstairs and into Mum's room and saw that she'd been tidying up in there as well. All of the jewellery and makeup that was usually sprawled across her dressing table had gone. The bed was made and a few cushions had been neatly arranged on top of the pillows. The pile of clothes that usually lay in one corner had all been put away. It looked much cleaner and fresher.

I found a green checked blanket stuffed at the bottom of Mum's wardrobe. I rolled it up as tightly as I could and put it in the bag on top of the food, torch and playing cards. I went downstairs and back out, crossing the street to Matthew's house. I guessed he'd still be at the high street with Jake so I was going to ask Sheila or Brian if I could borrow them. But Matthew answered the door.

"You're back already!" I said. "How was the high street?"

"It was OK," he said. He was continuously rubbing his right thumb against the back of his left hand. It was as if he was trying to get rid of an invisible spot. I had a feeling the trip to the shops had triggered his anxieties again. I wondered if he'd left Jake behind in the gaming shop, when he suddenly appeared behind him.

"Can I borrow your binoculars please?" I said. Matthew frowned.

"Er. Yeah. I guess so. Why do you want them?"

I hadn't prepared an answer. I had no idea why Hal wanted them either, but I guessed it had something to do with the stakeout and that it was highly important.

"Yeah, Melody," said Jake. "What do you want binoculars for? And what's in your bag?"

He tried to look but I moved the bag to one side. Fortunately, only the green checked blanket was showing.

"I'm . . . having a picnic," I said. "In the graveyard. And I thought I'd do some birdwatching while I was there."

I smiled. It all sounded perfectly feasible to me.

"A picnic? In a *graveyard*?" said Jake. "Weirdo."

He said it under his breath but it was loud enough for me to hear.

"I'll go and get them," said Matthew. He turned and went upstairs. His cat, Nigel, slunk around the front door, down the step and brushed against my legs.

"Hello, Nigel," I said, stroking his thick fur. Nigel purred deeply, enjoying the attention.

"Are you *seriously* having a picnic with all those rotten corpses around?" said Jake. "Don't you think that's a really, really odd thing to do?"

I thought about Hal, camping out in a disused building, and Martin Stone on the prowl with a gun hidden under his jacket. Jake had *no* idea how exciting this all was. I wished I could tell him, just to shut him up for once. But I couldn't. I was part of the team now and I had to be loyal to them.

"Yes I am. So what?" I said. Jake looked me up and down as if I was some kind of alien.

"You are seriously freaky," he said, shaking his head.

Matthew reappeared with the binoculars tucked under his arm. He held them out and I quickly took them.

"Thanks, Matty," I said, but Matthew was busy staring at something. A large, black car circled the close and pulled up outside Mr Charles's house.

"Look!" said Jake. "It's that woman!"

The engine turned off and Mr Charles's daughter, Melissa Dawson, climbed out. She was wearing dark sunglasses, a white shirt and a long, black skirt that reached down to her ankles. We hadn't seen her since last summer when her son, Teddy, went missing from Chestnut Close – the mystery that Matthew solved. When it happened, Melissa had been away for work and Mr Charles had been looking after the children.

"Are the kids with her too?" I whispered.

Melissa opened the back door of the car and a girl wearing a navy dress and white trainers jumped down on to the pavement.

"It's Casey," said Matthew, quietly. Casey was Teddy's older sister. She was a peculiar child and seemed to view everything through narrow eyes. She always looked like her brain was busy thinking of something evil to do. Melissa leaned into the car to release a seatbelt and a boy scrambled out. He was wearing smart trousers and a yellow checked shirt and in one hand he was holding a chunky plastic mobile phone. His once wispy, blonde hair was now a mop of curls.

"And there's Teddy," I said. "They've got so big!"

I was surprised how much older they looked but I guess ten months was a long time when you're little. Casey turned and stared at us. Her long hair was scraped back into a high ponytail which made her eyes look even more narrow.

"That kid is well creepy," said Jake, straining to see what was going on. For once I actually agreed with him about something.

"Welcome! Hello! Hello!" said Mr Charles, appearing from his front door. "It's been so *long*!" He walked down the pathway and embraced Melissa, who turned her cheek to one side. Teddy immediately ran indoors while Casey slunk behind Melissa's skirt.

"Hi, Dad," said Melissa. "Thank you so much for this. The school were fine about it, by the way. I told them it would just be a few days."

"Any time, darling," said Mr Charles. He walked to the boot of the car and took out two small suitcases. They all went inside number eleven and the door banged shut.

"I wonder if Melissa is travelling for work

again?" I said.

"Cor, you're *so* nosy, Melody," said Jake. "You're always trying to find out other people's business."

I glared at him. "No, I'm not!" I said.

"Yes, you are! You're always like 'oh where are you two off to?' You have to know *everything*," he said. "You're exhausting *and* nosy. Isn't she, Matthew?"

I looked at Matthew but he didn't make eye contact.

"Leave it, Jake," he said. But he said it so softly I don't think Jake heard.

I put the binoculars on top of the blanket in my bag and stormed off down the path. The door banged shut behind me.

I walked down the alleyway, the bag of supplies bumping against my leg. At least *Hal* needed me. *He* didn't think I was nosy or exhausting. I was part of his team! *And* I'd almost completed my first assignment. All that was missing were the clothes.

As I walked I looked over the low wall into Jake's garden. Jake's mum, Sue, was on the phone in the kitchen, emptying the dishwasher at the same time. On their patio was a rotary washing line filled with clothes. I spotted a grey hoodie that belonged to

Jake and a pair of his jeans. Hal might be older but he was skinny and around the same height as Jake. They could be perfect!

Sue had her back to the window. Then she walked out of the kitchen. It was now or never. I put the bag down and pulled myself up and over the wall. I ran to the washing, yanked the clothes off the line, making the pegs ping into the air, then bundled them under my arm. They felt dry at least. I quickly climbed back over the wall and stuffed them into the bag, then hurried on my way.

If Jake and Matthew wanted to leave me out then that was just fine with me – they were welcome to each other! Why would I want to be friends with them, anyway? Jake was horrible and Matthew was too spineless to stick up for me. I thought about Hal waiting in the plague house for me to return with food and some essential equipment. I had *far* more important things to do.

CHAPTER 14

Hal was waiting on the other side of the front door of the plague house. He spotted the bag immediately.

"Brilliant! I think you can say that you are now a part of the Warley Tower branch, Melody Bird," he said.

I grinned as I followed him into the back room.

Hal sat cross-legged on the blanket and I knelt down and began to empty the bag. I put the food in front of him.

"Amazing! I'm starving!" he said. He sandwiched a slice of cheese between two crackers. Crumbs fell down his red cardigan but he didn't bother to brush them away.

"You'll never guess what happened on my way home," I said. "I met Martin Stone! And he's got a gun!" Hal froze, the cracker sandwich posed in mid-air. His right eyelid flickered slightly.

"A ... gun?" he said. I nodded.

"You didn't communicate with him, did you?" he said.

"Yes!" I said. "By the tap."

"This is bad," Hal said. "What did you tell him? Did you mention me?"

"Of course not!" I said. "He told me he was watering the roses on his wife's grave. He said he has to come back every day to do it or they'll dry out and die."

Hal rubbed his forehead. He looked anxious. I was worried I'd done something wrong.

"At least you know that he'll be here every day to water. That's a good thing, isn't it?" I said.

"You can't believe a word he says," said Hal. "It's probably not even his wife's grave! He's a criminal, remember? And where was the gun, exactly?"

"In a holster under his jacket."

Hal looked confused. "You're absolutely certain?" he said. "You are one hundred per cent sure it was a gun?"

I thought for a moment. Had I really seen a gun? Or had I *thought* I'd seen a gun?

"I ... I ... think so," I said. I thought of the grey handle poking out of the top. "Yes, it was definitely a gun."

Hal nodded. "Things are developing quicker than I expected, then," he said. "It's going to heat up. We've got to be extra vigilant from now on, Melody Bird. Don't approach him again. I don't believe you are at risk, but *I* need to be very, very careful indeed."

I nodded and he carried on eating the crackers and cheese.

"Has there been any news from your team yet?" I said.

"No. The technical guys are on it, I'm sure," he said. "Did you manage to get everything?"

"Yes!" I said. I took the things out. "There are some clothes, a torch and the binoculars. Just like you asked."

He smiled. "Thank you, Melody Bird," he said. He spotted the pack of cards under Jake's hoodie and picked them up.

"Oh, yes. I brought those because I thought you might want to do some magic in your spare time," I said. "I imagine there's a lot of sitting around involved in a stakeout." Hal finished the crackers and tipped the cards into this hand. He began to shuffle them at lightning speed, cascading them from one palm to the other. It was incredible to watch.

"Let's try one right now, shall we?" he said. "This is called a 'snap'." He held the ace of hearts up between his fingers. "It's quite clever because when I snap my fingers, the card will miraculously change. Like ... this."

He snapped the fingers of his other hand and immediately the card he was holding changed into the seven of clubs.

I gasped.

"Wow! How did you do that?" I said.

Hal shuffled the cards again.

"I'm afraid a proper magician never reveals his tricks," he said. "It wouldn't be magic then, would it?"

He was right. Who wanted to know how a trick was done? That would only ruin it. He did the trick three more times and I still couldn't see how he was doing it. It was amazing! He put the cards down and held up Jake's hoodie.

"This is perfect," he said. He took off his red cardigan and put the hoodie on. It instantly made him look like anyone I'd see in town.

"It's Jake's," I said. "From his washing line. I kind of stole it. Not that I care."

"Ah. The notorious Jake," said Hal, shuffling the cards again. "And how's Matthew?"

I shrugged. "He's OK, I guess," I said. "Jake's over at Matthew's house right now. They hang out a lot, like I said."

Hal nodded and carefully slid the cards back into the box. "And what about you? Who do you hang out with?" he said.

I swallowed and stared at his grey blanket. It had a thin, yellow ribbon stitched along the edge. It looked a bit like the kind of blanket you had when you were a baby.

"I don't hang out with anyone really. That's fine though. I like my own company." I got up off the blanket.

"Are you lonely, Melody?" Hal said. "Like Mr Charles?"

"What? No!" I said. "Of course not!" I smiled, but it was the kind of smile that made my face ache a little. He was watching me, closely.

"Anyway, I'd better go now," I said. "I need to take Frankie for a walk."

Hal looked at me and frowned.

"Can you come back tomorrow?" he said. "I think ... I think I might have something I need your help with. A mission. It's totally confidential, of course."

My heart skipped a beat. "A mission? Really?" I said.

Hal smiled. "Yes, if you think you're up to it."

I smiled back. Whatever it was, I was sure I could handle it. "Sure. That sounds good," I said. "I'll see you tomorrow!"

CHAPTER 15

The next day was Sunday. Every Sunday morning, Mum and I took Frankie for a walk together. We'd start off on the high street, where Mum would buy a newspaper and a coffee, then we'd do a loop of the town park before heading home. It was a long walk for Frankie and sometimes we took it in turns to carry him on the way home if he'd had enough.

This Sunday, however, Mum said she had more important things to do. Like clearing out our shed.

"I'm sorry, Melody. Can you take Frankie out on your own?" she said, over breakfast. "I've got so much to do this weekend. The estate agent has booked more viewings in next week. It's all happening so quickly!"

She seemed pleased. I certainly wasn't.

"Why are you bothering?" I said. "I've told you. I am *not* moving."

Mum sighed. "Melody," she said. "There's no need to be like that."

"Like what?" I said. I put down my toast. "You lied to me, Mum. You put the house up for sale and you lied!"

"I did not lie! I just hadn't got around to telling you in time!" shouted Mum.

I took a long breath. "You made a decision without me. You talked to an estate agent. You arranged to sell the house. You lied!" I said. "You're no different to Dad."

I saw Mum flinch when I said that and I almost wished I could take it back. Comparing her to Dad was harsh, but then it wasn't me who hadn't been telling the truth.

"This is my home, Mum. MY HOME," I said. "And I am staying here."

Mum was breathing hard. She didn't look angry any more though; she looked upset. We stared at each other for a few seconds, then I got up and went out of the kitchen. I put Frankie on his lead and slammed the door so hard the windows rattled.

Not going for a walk with Mum suited me just fine. Now I could go straight to the plague house and find out exactly what Hal's mission for me entailed. It was so exciting!

Frankie and I did our usual circuit of the graveyard and I kept a look out for Martin Stone but I didn't see him. We headed through the weeds to the plague house. Hal was waiting for us. He looked cheerful.

"You're back!" he said. "And you've brought the furry sausage with you!"

I giggled as Frankie scampered towards him. His little bottom scooted from left to right as he wagged his tail. Hal crouched down and tickled him behind his ears.

"Hello, boy," he said. "You're so cute, aren't you?"

We went through to the back room and Frankie flopped on to Hal's blanket for a snooze.

"So, what's the mission?" I said. "I've been wondering all morning what it could be!"

Hal grinned and went over to his rucksack, unzipping a pocket on the front. He took out a small piece of folded paper and passed it to me.

"There has been a major development in the case," he said. "At last, the work I've been doing here is beginning to pay off. I think that *this* could lead us to the Kingfisher Necklace." He began to unfold the piece of paper. "I've intercepted a message. It's almost certainly been left by Martin Stone, trying to communicate with an associate."

He passed the piece of paper to me. The note was handwritten, the letters curly and neat. I read what it said out loud:

> Use me wisely and I am somebody.
> Turn me round and I am nobody.

I looked at Hal.

"Where did you find it?" I said.

Hal was looking out of the window. "It was on the grave that Martin Stone visits. He must have left it there for someone to collect."

I read the message again. "What do you think it means?" I said.

"I've no idea. I'd usually feed this one back to the team to work on. But that's not going to be possible right now," he said, holding up his wrist with his broken watch. "I was thinking *you* might like to take this on as a mission, Melody Bird."

"Really?!" I said. My stomach did a flip-flop of excitement.

"Really!" he said.

He looked utterly serious. This was brilliant! I *loved* solving things!

"So, what do you think?" he said. "Any ideas?"

I read the note again, trying to look professional. "Um. Well, it sounds like a riddle," I said.

"I agree," said Hal.

I frowned as I thought hard.

"Use me wisely . . . what do we use wisely?" I said. "Does it mean like a knife or something dangerous? Use me wisely in case you cut yourself?"

Hal just shrugged. I *had* to solve it so that he'd be pleased he'd asked me to join the team. I really wanted to impress him.

"Did you know that the word 'riddle' comes from the word 'read'?" I said. "Riddles have been found that are *thousands* of years old."

Hal laughed. "I did not know that," he said. "I love interesting facts like that."

"Me too!" I said, grinning.

"I've got one that's perfect for a graveyard," he

said. "Did you know that they would reuse coffins in Georgian times?"

"Really?" I said. A shiver ran down my back.

Hal nodded. "They waited until the body had rotted away, and they would dig up the coffin, tip the bones out and resell it."

"That is *so* creepy," I said. "What are you going to do with the note? Won't someone be looking for it?"

Hal nodded. "Yes. I need to put it back on the grave so that it's not missed. Martin Stone usually comes in the afternoon. Do you want to copy the riddle down?"

I read it one more time and passed it back to him. "I'll remember it," I said. "I just need some time to think it over."

"Brilliant," said Hal. "I knew I could rely on you."

"I'd better get Frankie home, but I'll be back tomorrow after school," I said. "I'll bring you some more food as well."

"Thank you, Melody Bird," he said with a smile. "You're the best."

I stayed in my room for most of the evening. Mum suggested that we watched a film together but I said I didn't want to. I almost felt bad – she looked so sad when I said no – but then I remembered the FOR SALE sign wobbling on our driveway.

That night, the riddle went round and round in my head. *Use me wisely and I am somebody, Turn me round and I am nobody.*

How could you be "somebody" and then "nobody"? It didn't make any sense.

When I closed my eyes all I could see was Hal, alone in the dark in the cold, creepy plague house. Did he get the note back in time? I imagined Martin Stone arriving with his gun hidden beneath his jacket. What if he discovered Hal? I *had* to solve this riddle, but it felt impossible.

The clock on my bedside table said two a.m. I decided to go downstairs to get a glass of water. When I got to the bottom step, though, I stopped.

I had seen something moving in the close through the frosted glass of our door. I went to the lounge and peeked through the gap in the curtains. Someone was standing in the shadows at the end of the alleyway. They were doing a good job of keeping out of sight, but I could see enough to tell they were holding up a pair of binoculars. They turned to look slowly up and down the street, inspecting each house in turn: Jake's first, then the Jenkins', then

Matthew's, then Mr Charles's. Then the person put the binoculars down and I saw his face.

It was Hal. He was wearing Jake's hoodie and jeans with Matthew's binoculars round his neck. He lifted them and focused on number one – the house that was empty – and then he slowly turned the binoculars towards my house. I ducked out the way and waited a few seconds, then looked back again. He'd moved on and was studying the windows of the Rectory now. He spent a long time with the binoculars trained on the Rectory and I wondered what he was so interested in – the single lamp that Old Nina had glowing in her window, or the bushes beneath her window that covered an old cellar. He put the binoculars down, took a final look around the close, then disappeared back into the darkness.

It seemed like he was looking for something ... or some*one*? Maybe that someone was the master criminal, Martin Stone? Maybe the dangerous criminal was hiding out on the close!

"What are you up to Hal?" I whispered.

I went to the kitchen to get a glass of water. Frankie lifted his head from his little bed down by the fridge then laid back down again. As I walked past the dining room a glint of something caught my eye – a sliver of light reflecting off the mirror that I had helped Mum to hang on the wall just the other day. I stared at it and thought of Hal's riddle in my head.

> *Use me wisely and I am somebody.*
> *Turn me round and I am nobody.*

The answer was a mirror! Now I knew the answer it seemed so obvious. I went back up to bed and dived under my duvet, grinning to myself. I'd solved the riddle – and finished my mission already!

CHAPTER 16

I couldn't wait to tell Hal that I'd solved the riddle – but first I had school.

School went really slowly like it always did when I wanted to be doing something else. In the morning I had English, Science and French. Matthew was in all of my lessons and we said hello, but I didn't make any effort to talk to him. Why should I? He clearly preferred Jake's company to mine. Besides, I was too busy thinking. What did a *mirror* mean? What did it have to do with the mysterious missing necklace?

Now that Matthew was hanging out with Jake, I didn't have anyone to sit with at lunchtime. I ate my sandwiches in a corner of the canteen then headed to the library to finish some homework. After half an hour the bell went for next lesson which was PE. I came out of the library and Jake and Matthew were waiting for me in the corridor.

"Melody! Have you got a spare pair of trainers with you? Or shorts? Or a top?" said Jake.

"No," I said. "Why? What's happened?"

"Jake has forgotten his PE kit again," said Matthew.

This was not good. We had rounders on the field with Mr Jenkins now. If it was any other teacher Jake would probably just get a negative mark, but there was no knowing what Mr Jenkins might do.

"Ask someone else?" I said.

"I've asked everyone!" said Jake. He looked upset. I couldn't help but feel sorry for him.

"How about asking your mum or dad to bring it in?" said Matthew. "We could get the office to call them now."

"Mum's at work and Dad lives too far away to get here in time," said Jake. "And anyway, the lesson starts *now*. It's too late. I'm dead."

"Just be honest and tell Mr Jenkins you're really sorry but you just forgot," I said. "Tell him that it's not an excuse not to play, you were looking forward to rounders and you want to join in wearing your school uniform."

Jake thought about it. His face brightened a little.

"Yeah ... maybe. He can't get angry if I'm still willing to take part, can he? He'll know I didn't do it on purpose to get out of the lesson."

"Exactly," I said.

Jake looked a bit more cheerful. He and Matthew went off to the sports hall and I followed behind them.

When I got to the changing room I found a space in a corner. Beside me were Carrie and Monique. I quickly changed into my PE kit and kept my head down. Everyone around me was chatting and giggling about something that had happened on social media but I didn't know what they were talking about. I sat down to tie my trainers. Carrie was brushing her hair and tying it back in a ponytail and Monique was putting on some lip gloss using her phone as a mirror, even though we weren't allowed to have our phones out during school hours. She glanced at me over her screen and I smiled. She smiled back but didn't say anything.

The girls in my year weren't ever horrible to me but I think this was because, to them, I was invisible.

Sometimes it even felt like they were looking right *through* me. I was just of no interest. That was absolutely fine with me, I didn't *want* to be a part of their 'lip-gloss' world. I had Frankie and the graveyard, and Hal, and my very own spy mission.

I stuffed my uniform into my bag to make sure nothing got lost or taken and hung it on a hook before heading out to the field. Mr Jenkins was marking out a rounders pitch using some plastic cones. A few of the boys spilled out of the other changing room. I spotted Matthew but there was no sign of Jake. I went over.

"What happened?" I said. "Did Mr Jenkins let him off?"

Matthew looked white. "Not exactly. He said he's got to take part and told him to find something to wear."

My stomach churned on Jake's behalf.

"Not the lost property bin?" I said. In the corridor outside the changing rooms was a bright-blue bin filled to the top with muddy socks, ripped rugby tops and odd trainers. It stank of mould when you walked past it. Anything in there would be utterly disgusting.

"It's worse than that," said Matthew. "Mr

Jenkins said there was nothing appropriate in lost property. He went and got a box ... from the drama department."

"The *drama* department?" I said. "But ... that means he'd have to wear ..." I stopped. The chatter of students around us had suddenly gone deathly silent. The door to the boy's changing room slowly opened and Jake appeared, squinting in the bright sun. There was an audible gasp.

"Oh no," I said.

Jake was wearing grey tights and his body was covered by a large, cardboard box painted silver. His arms jutted out at awkward angles. He was wearing the Tin-Man costume from last winter's school production of The Wizard of Oz.

"What's he got that on for?" said Lyla.

"Hey! Jake!" called Joseph. "The yellow brick road is that way!"

Matthew and I rushed over to him.

"It was either this or Dorothy's dress," he said. His face had that tight look, when you know someone is trying not to cry. As much as he'd been mean to me, seeing him humiliated was awful.

"Don't let him beat you," I said, firmly. "Hold your head high and pretend not to be bothered. OK?"

"Melody's right," said Matthew. "And we're on your side."

Jake nodded. Then he turned to the rest of the class and grinned. "Has anyone got an oil can?" he yelled.

There were a few sniggers from the rest of the class but they stopped when Mr Jenkins walked over, pounding a rounders bat into the palm of his hand.

"You took your time, Jake," he said. "Maybe next time you'll think twice about 'forgetting' your kit, eh? Right, get into teams you lot. Let's play."

Jake couldn't run very fast in a giant cardboard box and everyone laughed at him; on the plus side, he was out pretty quickly. This meant sitting on the side in the baking sun. When it was Jake's team's turn to field he stayed right at the other end of the pitch where it was unlikely for the ball to end up. Whenever I looked his way, I thought his eyes looked dazed. It was like his body was here, but in his head he'd gone somewhere else: to a place where he wasn't being humiliated by a teacher.

PE was the last lesson of the day. I hurried to get

changed and caught up with Matthew and Jake as they headed home. Jake was pushing his bike beside Matthew and they were walking in silence.

"Are you OK?" I said to Jake.

Jake just shrugged and stared down at the ground.

"Well, I thought you were brilliant this afternoon," I said. Matthew brightened a little.

"Yeah, you kept your cool. I bet Mr Jenkins was wound up about that," he said.

"For sure. He was probably livid!" I said.

"He's not going to get away with it," said Jake, quietly.

Matthew looked over at me, concern on his face. "Just leave it, Jake. You won't win against someone like Mr Jenkins."

Jake shook his head. His eyes were red and so was the tip of his nose. "I'll get my own back, one day," he said.

He wiped his face on his sleeve then jumped on his bike and pedalled away.

We watched him go. Mr Jenkins had it in for Jake. We all knew it and I think even the teachers did too, but Jake had a reputation for being a troublemaker and so they mostly turned a blind eye. I think the other teachers were also a bit scared of Mr Jenkins. I'd never seen anyone stand up to him. That is, apart from Mrs Chambers – our teacher in Year Six. And that was how the whole thing had begun...

A few times a year our high school would host sports competitions for the local, younger schools. The high school has brilliant sport facilities and their older students would help to organize the day for the younger kids. One spring, when we were still in primary school, a basketball tournament was organized and our Year Six class was invited to take part. Our teacher, Mrs Chambers, asked for volunteers and ten of us were chosen, including me and Jake. Matthew didn't put his hand up. I think he was quite happy to stay in the classroom.

When it was time for us to leave, the ten of us waited by the school gates wearing our PE kits. Mrs Chambers appeared from the office carrying Jake's yellow medical bag. The bag contained the emergency supplies needed should he accidentally come in contact with something that could cause an allergic reaction, like a peanut or a prawn.

"Right, I want everyone walking in pairs," said Mrs Chambers. She headed to the front of the line. "Jake, if you get too hot and your skin flares up you must let me know, OK?" He nodded to her.

"All right, Team Squirrels! Let's go and shoot some hoops!" She waved Jake's bag like it was a cheerleader's pompom and we all whooped. We loved Mrs Chambers. She was always jolly and made our lessons fun, even if she had come up with a ridiculous name for our team.

It was a twenty-minute walk to the high school and the final ten minutes were up a steep hill. Mrs Chambers wasn't particularly fit and she found it quite a struggle.

"Go ahead. Just wait ... for me ... at the gate..." she said, as we all overtook her. She stopped for a moment and rested her hands on the top of her thighs, breathing hard.

"If she doesn't hurry up we're going to miss the first game," said Tom. He took our high school sports afternoons seriously. We watched as Mrs Chambers edged up the hill towards us. Her face was red and there were two sweat patches seeping into her blouse from under her arms.

"Goodness. That was quite the climb," she said

when she finally reached us. "Right! Let's go and play ball!"

The tournament went like it always did when we took part in events like these – by the time we got to the last game, we were right at the bottom of the league. We weren't a very sporty class. We all sat slumped and sweaty in the corner of the hall. There was still one game to go.

"You've all been marvellous!" said Mrs Chambers.

"We're last," said Tom.

"You've still been marvellous! And as you know, it's the taking part that counts!"

We didn't know Mr Jenkins back then. He was just the PE teacher in charge of the event, although we'd quickly worked out that he was tough and didn't stand for any nonsense. He walked over to us, consulting a black clipboard.

"Team Squirrels, you're in last place," he said. He tucked his clipboard under his arm and crouched down in front of us. "So, what are you going to do about it?"

We stared at him and Mrs Chambers chuckled.

"What they are going to *do*, Mr Jenkins, is enjoy taking part in the final match. Isn't that right, Team Squirrels?" she said.

We blinked up at her, and then back at Mr Jenkins. His lip seemed to have curled up slightly.

"Anyway, you're up against the Dragons now," he said, ignoring her. "Look sharp and put some effort into it." He stood up, took a silver whistle out of his top pocket and blasted it, making us and Mrs Chambers jump.

We slowly got to our feet.

Mrs Chambers chose five of us for the team and we dragged ourselves to the middle of the court.

Mr Jenkins refereed the match and every time anyone did something wrong he gave a sharp *PEEEEEEPPPP!* on his whistle and pointed at them. He was particularly tough on Jake, who I could tell was really trying. Tom managed to get two hoops but when the final whistle blew we lost 34–4. The other team cheered and one of their players threw the ball high up into the air in celebration. Mr Jenkins went around, patting each of them on the back. Mrs Chambers came on to the court and surprised us by catching the plummeting ball.

"Well done, Squirrels! Well done!" she said. "You gave it your best shot!"

Mr Jenkins laughed.

"I'm not sure congratulations are in order, Mrs

Chambers. Your team lost every single match. Do you really think praise is due?"

Mrs Chambers tucked the basketball under her arm and took a step closer to Mr Jenkins. He took a slight step backwards.

"I disagree, Mr Jenkins," she said. "I think my Squirrels did well today. They didn't give up. They showed resilience. Losing is sometimes a good lesson in life, don't you think?"

Mr Jenkins chuckled. "Well, I wouldn't know about that, personally," he said.

"Oh? Have you always been a winner, Mr Jenkins?" Mrs Chambers said. "Have you never come last in anything at all?"

Mr Jenkins frowned as if he was thinking and then he shrugged.

"Nope. Some people are just born winners, I guess," he said. He looked her up and down as she stared back at him. The sports hall began to hush as the other teams and teachers realized something was going on. Mrs Chambers nodded at Mr Jenkins, then she began to thump the basketball on to the floor.

Once.

Twice.

Three times.

"Oh no. She isn't . . . is she?" whispered Jake.

Mr Jenkins watched her as she bounced the ball. He seemed to be finding it amusing.

"This might be hard for you to believe, Mr Jenkins, but I used to be quite useful on a basketball court back in the day," said Mrs Chambers.

Mr Jenkins laughed.

"It *is* hard to believe that, yes," he said, folding his arms and tipping his head to one side.

Mrs Chambers bounced the ball again.

Four.

Five.

Six.

The thumps echoed around the hall.

"How about we shoot some hoops, just you and me?" said Mrs Chambers.

Mr Jenkins frowned.

"I'm sorry?" he said, incredulously.

"Best of five?" said Mrs Chambers. "Come on, what do you say?"

Mr Jenkins stared at her as she began to circle him. They looked like two cowboys, waiting to see who was going to draw first.

"I wouldn't want to humiliate you," he said, quietly.

Mrs Chambers didn't even blink.

"I think I can take it," she said. Our class whooped and cheered and Mr Jenkins darted a look at us.

"OK, if you insist. Best of five," he said.

Everyone in the hall gathered around the hoop in a big semicircle as the contest began. Mr Jenkins said that Mrs Chambers could go first.

"Come on, Mrs Chambers. You can do it!" said Jake. She gave him a smile before making her way to the free-throw line. She stuck her tongue out a little as she concentrated, then she sent the ball up into the air. It was a weak throw and it didn't reach anywhere near the hoop. Team Squirrels groaned.

"AND IT'S A MISS," yelled Mr Jenkins. Mrs Chambers turned to us and gave us a big smile.

Mr Jenkins was up next. He walked to the line and threw the ball without any hesitation. It went straight in.

"ONE–NIL," he shouted. There was a smattering of applause.

"Come on, Mrs Chambers!" said Samira in our team. "You can do it!"

Our teacher nodded at her then took her position. She threw the ball again harder. This time it hit the back board, hit the edge of the hoop and bounced out.

"Oh, that was close!" said Jake.

Mrs Chambers and Mr Jenkins swapped places and again. Mr Jenkins threw the ball and scored.

"TWO–NIL! Mrs Chambers, you're up."

She walked to the line and bounced the ball in front of her. Excited chatter began to fill the hall and then Jake began to clap.

"SHOOT THE HOOP! SHOOT THE HOOP! SHOOT THE HOOP!" he shouted, slapping his hands together at the same time.

The rest of Team Squirrels joined in and before long, the entire hall was chanting. Mr Jenkins looked around. His face was like a threatening cloud just before you heard a rumble of thunder.

Mrs Chambers walked to the line, ready to shoot. A hush descended around the hall. Everyone was completely silent as she threw the ball. It wavered in the air and sunk straight through the hoop.

Everyone erupted, clapping, cheering and banging their feet on the floor. The sound was absolutely deafening. It was as if Mrs Chambers had just won an Olympic gold medal.

"TWO–ONE," yelled Mr Jenkins, above the

cheers. He walked to the line, thumping the ball with extra force on to the ground. He waited for everyone to quieten down.

"If I get this in, then I'm afraid it's game over," he called out. He turned back, ready to shoot. There was a collective intake of air as everyone held their breath. He bounced the ball once, twice and then jumped as he threw it. The ball soared into the air and sank through the hoop, barely touching the edges.

He'd won.

"YES! GET IN!" said Mr Jenkins. He punched the air three times, then held his arms out to the crowd.

But the crowd were silent. There were no cheers, no applause, no stamping of feet. Nothing. He looked around in disbelief and then his eyes fixed on Jake. The small boy, red with eczema, who had started the chant.

Mrs Chambers turned to us and smiled.

"Come on, Team Squirrels," she said. "It's time to go home."

CHAPTER 17

I went straight from school to the plague house. I couldn't wait to tell Hal that I'd solved the riddle and talk to him about what the answer might mean for the case.

But he wasn't there. The pebble was still on the windowsill and his belongings were in the corner of the room, but Hal was nowhere to be seen.

I walked over to where Hal's things were. The plastic bag that I'd brought yesterday now had the empty tubs and wrappers put neatly inside it. His rucksack was wide open. I glanced around, and then I took a look.

His red, woolly cardigan was folded up on the top

and I reached my hand in and moved it to one side. I could see a small white envelope, some pencils, a notepad and the broken communication device.

I carefully pulled it out by the strap. The screen was blank and had a tiny crack across the middle. It looked just like an old-fashioned digital watch to me – but that was probably intentional. I guessed that if it was too flash and expensive-looking it would attract attention.

I tapped on the face and gently pressed a couple of the buttons on the sides. Nothing happened. It was completely dead. I was just turning it over to look at the back, when Hal walked in.

"What are you doing?" he said. He hurried over and zipped his rucksack closed. Then he saw that I still had the watch in my hand.

"You mustn't touch that," he said. I held it out and he snatched it from me.

"Sorry. I was just seeing if I could get it working," I said. "Do you want me to take it to the jewellers on the high street? They might be able to help."

Hal put the watch back on his wrist. "No," he said, firmly. "This watch stays with me."

"OK," I said. "I was only offering. Hey, guess what? I solved the riddle!"

"Really?" he said, brightening up.

"Yes! The answer is a mirror! If you use it wisely, then you can see your reflection, but if you turn it round then you can't see yourself. You're nobody!"

Hal smiled and shook his head. "A mirror. I would never have figured that one out. That's brilliant. Well done, Melody Bird!"

I relaxed a little. Hal was right. I shouldn't have been snooping through his things. We were a team now.

"What do you think a 'mirror' means?" I said. "What does it have to do with the case?"

Hal chewed on his bottom lip.

"I'm not sure yet," he admitted. "But it looks like it's just the start. I was at the grave just now and found this."

He took a square piece of paper out of the pocket of Jake's hoodie. It looked identical to the first one.

"Another riddle!" I said. He handed it to me. I opened it up and read.

When you need me, you throw me away.
When you're finished with me, you take me in.

I wrinkled my nose. It was a tough one.

"Why would you throw something away when you needed it? It doesn't make sense," I said.

"I know. They're very clever, this gang," said Hal. "*And* fast. They managed to collect the other note without me seeing. But that doesn't matter. It's Stone we are interested in and the whereabouts of the necklace. Not them."

I thought really hard about the riddle. I pictured myself using something by throwing it away. A boomerang? No. That didn't fit with the second line.

"This is so frustrating," I said. "I know Matthew would probably solve it in seconds!"

Hal looked alarmed. "No! You can't tell Matthew!" he said.

"I won't," I reassured him. "I'm just saying he's got one of those brains that can work puzzles out really quickly, that's all."

I looked back at the piece of paper.

"There's something about these messages I don't understand," I said. "Why are they writing notes to each other in code? Why don't they text or phone or email each other?"

Hal smiled. "You know the saying about something being *right under your nose*? Or *hidden in plain sight*? Sometimes the simple ideas are the ones that are the most overlooked. We can trace a phone call or a text message from miles away."

I thought about when I'd first met Hal and thought he looked nothing like a spy. He had said that was on purpose. He was the last person you'd suspect.

"It's a bit like a bluff in a magic trick," said Hal. "You know, when a magician leads you to think that the trick has gone wrong and that he really doesn't know where your card is, and then, bam – they turn over a playing card that you weren't watching and it's *your* card! *That's* the magical moment. When it's totally unexpected."

"That makes sense," I said.

"The investigation is going well, Melody," Hal said. "At the moment Martin Stone doesn't realize we've found these messages. We're one step ahead." He sat down by the window and stared out towards the cemetery. "I'm pretty certain that these messages are being left for an unknown accomplice to lead them to the hiding place of the Kingfisher Necklace. If we can piece them together and find out where it's hidden, *then* we can make our move."

It all sounded so exciting. "Shall I put the note back now?" I said. "In case the accomplice turns up?"

Hal stood up. "No. It's too dangerous," he said. "You're risking enough as it is by helping me. I'll take it back."

"Hang on. I'll take a photo," I said. I took out my mobile and took a quick picture, then handed the note back to Hal. He looked at me, wide eyed.

I stared back at him. "What is it?" I said. "Have I done something wrong?"

He quickly shook his head.

"No. It's fine," he said.

"I'll come back later with Frankie and I'll bring you some food," I said.

Hal smiled at me. "Thanks, Melody Bird. You're brilliant," he said.

I smiled back at him. Being on a team felt really good.

I thought about the riddle on my walk home.

"When you need me, you throw me away. When you're finished with me, you take me in." I came out of the alleyway and on to my road. "What does it mean?" I muttered.

"Hello, Melody!" It was Matthew's dad, Brian. He was standing on his driveway resting his elbows on the roof of his car. Their front door was wide open.

"Hi, Brian," I said. I walked over.

"Just waiting for Matthew, as usual," said Brian.

It was time for Matthew's appointment with Dr Rhodes which he had every Monday. Her office was on the high street.

"We're sorry to see you and your mum are moving," Brian said, nodding towards the FOR SALE sign outside our house.

"We're not moving now," I said. "Mum is going to get the sign taken down."

Brian gave me a slow nod. "I see," he said gently. "I haven't seen you over here lately," he added. "Everything all right with you and Matthew?"

I wanted to say that actually, it wasn't, because Matthew clearly preferred the company of Jake now and it was very hurtful. But I didn't.

"Everything's fine," I said. Brian looked at his watch and bellowed towards the open door.

"HURRY UP, MATTHEW!" He looked back at me. "I don't want to be late for my quiz later."

Brian was the captain of a pub quiz team called

"Brian's Brains". They travelled around the county taking part in competitions.

I suddenly had an idea.

"Do you know much about riddles, Brian?" I said. He perked up a bit.

"Hmmm. They're not my area of expertise," he said. "But try me! I'm always happy to give it a go." He rubbed his hands together.

"OK. Well, it goes like this," I said. I cleared my throat. "*When you use me, you throw me away. When you're finished with me, you take me in.*"

Brian's forehead creased and his eyes shut. He looked like he'd gone into some kind of trance. It must have been his thinking face. A few times he opened his mouth as though he was about to say something, but then closed it again and shook his head. It seemed to have stumped him as well. Matthew came out and banged the door shut behind him.

"At last!" said Brian, opening the driver's door. "Come on, son. We're going to be late."

Brian climbed into the car as Matthew walked around to the passenger side. Matthew looked worried, I thought.

"Hi, Matthew. Are you OK?" I said. He slowly nodded.

"Dr Rhodes is going to do more practical stuff with me this week," he said.

I knew what that meant. Matthew had told me about it in the past. Dr Rhodes would pick things that Matthew was scared of, like a bin lid or the bottom of his shoe. He had to be as brave as possible and touch them and try not to immediately wash his hands. It was a process called "exposure and response" therapy. His whole body looked stiff with fear.

He used the cuff of his shirt to open the car door. Even though he'd been ignoring me lately, my heart ached to see him like that. He looked utterly terrified.

"You'll be OK, Matthew," I said. "You're doing brilliantly. Look how far you've come!"

He gave me a weak smile, then got in and closed the car door. Brian began to reverse out of the driveway as I walked along the pavement towards home. He pulled up alongside me and his window went down.

"Melody! I've got it!" he said. "The answer to your riddle. It's an anchor!"

He grinned at me, then drove off down the road.

An anchor! Of course! You throw an anchor

overboard when you need to use it, and you bring it back on to the ship when you don't need it any more. It was a genius riddle! I couldn't *wait* to tell Hal.

CHAPTER 18

When I got inside, I found Mum was sitting at the kitchen table looking at her laptop. I could see an estate agent's website up on her screen.

"Hello, love! You're a bit late home today. Is everything all right?" she asked.

"Yeah, I had something to do," I said. I knew she was waiting for me to say what it was but I kept quiet.

"I thought we could look at a few houses before dinner?" she said. "I've found some really nice places!"

"I'm not moving, Mum. You can't make me," I said.

I decided I'd make Hal a sandwich so I took some ham out of the fridge. Was he a vegetarian? He might be. I put it back and took out some cheese instead.

"Please, don't be like that, Melody," said Mum. "I just want us to be happy and—"

The doorbell went and Frankie trotted into the hallway, wagging his tail. Mum took a long breath then went to open the door.

I peered into the hallway. It was Mr Charles, with Casey and Teddy. Casey was holding some pieces of paper.

"Claudia!" said Mr Charles. "I was so sad to see you're moving. I hope you're not going far?"

Mum said something too quiet for me to hear.

"Doggy!" screeched Teddy. He wrenched his hand free from Mr Charles and ran straight into the house, plonking himself down on the carpet to pet Frankie.

"Teddy! Come back here!" said Mr Charles.

"Oh, don't worry. He's fine. Frankie loves a bit of fuss," said Mum. "What have you got there, Casey? A flier?"

I quickly wrapped up the sandwich for Hal and put it in a paper bag along with some fruit, two nut bars, a carton of juice and crisps. I headed to the hall.

"Is it this Saturday?" Mum said. She was looking at one of the pieces of paper that Casey was holding.

"Yes," said Mr Charles. "I know you're moving now but we'd love it if you'd both come. It'll be nice to have everyone coming together for the common good."

Frankie had rolled on to his back so that Teddy could tickle his tummy.

"Hello, doggy," said Teddy. "You're a lovely doggy. Funny doggy!"

Casey didn't say anything, just glared. I took Frankie's lead off the hook by the door. When he heard it jingle, Frankie flipped back on to his feet and trotted over.

"Look, Melody," said Mum, holding the flier. "There's a big clear-up in the graveyard on Saturday. We'll lend a hand, won't we?"

"In the graveyard?" My heart began to bang against my chest. Mum passed me the flier and I read it for myself.

THE BIG GRAVEYARD CLEAR-UP!
JOIN YOUR NEIGHBOURS ON SATURDAY, 9th
MAY AT 10AM
AND HELP TO TIDY ST JOSEPH'S CHURCH
GRAVEYARD.
REFRESHMENTS WILL BE PROVIDED.
BRING YOUR OWN
GARDENING GLOVES, PRUNING SHEARS ETC.
FOR ALL ENQUIRIES CONTACT
MR CHARLES AT
11 CHESTNUT CLOSE.

"But ... but that's a stupid idea!" I said. "The graveyard doesn't need a clear up!"

"Melody!" said Mum. "Don't be so rude."

"We won't be doing anything drastic," said Mr Charles, smiling, "Just tidying some of the pathways so that people can walk everywhere easily and cutting back the ivy that's been growing into Nina's garden."

I swallowed away the sick feeling that I now felt in my throat. If there were a load of people in the graveyard on Saturday, they might find Hal. Mum and Mr Charles started talking about who might be up for helping and I quickly put my shoes on. I waited for Teddy to give Frankie a final pat, then picked up his lead and headed out.

I ran through the graveyard, clutching the flier and the paper bag full of food to my chest. Frankie sprinted as fast as his little legs would go.

I burst into the plague house. Hal was sitting on the blankets with the playing cards in four piles in front of him.

"Hal! We have a problem!" I gasped.

"What is it?" he said, jumping up. "Is it Martin Stone?" He ran to the window and looked left and right.

"No, it's nothing like that," I said, putting the bag of food down. "But look!"

I passed him the flier.

He studied it in silence. I watched as his chest rose and fell. He rubbed his forehead and handed it back to me. "I guess I'll just have to move on," he said.

"Move on? But what about the case? Won't you be letting the Warley Tower branch down?" I said.

Hal paused for a moment.

"You're right," he said at last. "We've come so far in the case that to walk away now would be madness. I'll relocate, somewhere close, and continue the investigation."

I tried to think of somewhere he could go. We had a spare bedroom, but there was no way Hal could go undetected in there. Especially with Frankie sniffing around and the people viewing the house.

"Of course! I know exactly where you should go, and it's not far at all!" I said. Hal raised his eyebrows.

"Number one Chestnut Close!" I said. "It's right next door to me! And it's completely empty. You can stay there. No one will know. You'll have to keep the lights off and out of sight of the windows but it'll be safe for a few days. Mr Charles goes inside to check it every now and then, but he's only just done that so he won't be back for a while."

Hal seemed to relax a little.

"Do you really think it'll be OK?" he said.

"Yes! It's the perfect plan," I said.

"Do you think there's . . . a shower?"

I shrugged. "I guess so. Although there might not be any hot water."

"It sounds perfect," said Hal. "At least until I can make contact with Warley Tower."

"There's only one problem," I said. "I don't have a key. Mr Charles has the only one."

Hal's shoulders sagged. "OK. Never mind. It was a good idea," he said.

"You can still stay there!" I said. "I just need to come up with a plan to get hold of it."

Hal laughed. "Ha! You're brilliant, Melody Bird. There I was, all ready to give up straight away, but you're going to come up with a plan," he said. It was nice to be appreciated for a change.

That reminded me.

"And I solved the next riddle! Well, actually Matthew's dad, Brian, solved it. He's really into quizzing and I told him it was a riddle I'd read. Don't worry, I didn't give you away."

"Is there anything you *can't* do, Melody Bird?" Hal said, grinning. I felt my cheeks flush pink.

"Anyway, the answer is an anchor," I said.

Hal thought about it and then nodded. "Of course."

"So that's a mirror and an anchor," I said. "I think it must have something to do with the cemetery, don't you? Maybe a mirror and an anchor are carved into a headstone and that is where the Kingfisher Necklace is buried! Although, I've never seen any carvings like that and I know the graveyard better than anyone."

"I'm not sure," said Hal thoughtfully. "They seem to be leading to objects though, I agree. Let's see if another note appears, don't you think?"

I nodded, copying his thoughtful expression. Hal began to take the food out of the bag and beamed when he saw the sandwich. I liked helping people. It made me feel warm inside.

"Right. I'd better get on to my next mission," I said. "Getting the key to number one! I'll see you soon, Hal."

"See you soon, Melody Bird."

While Frankie and I walked home I tried to think of a plan. I came up with two options:

1) Tell Mr Charles that I'd heard a strange noise inside number one and could I borrow the key to check inside.
2) Tell Mr Charles I'd brought Frankie over to say hello to Teddy. Then I'd steal the key.

The trouble with option one is that I knew that Mr Charles would immediately want to go and investigate the noise himself. There was no way he'd just hand the key over.

Option two was also tricky. I would probably be invited in, but it was highly unlikely that I'd get a chance to go searching for the key. That is, unless I had someone to distract everyone while I snuck off. Which led me to option three.

   3) I go over with Frankie and someone creates a diversion which leads Mr Charles, Casey and Teddy outside, giving me time to find and pocket the key.

That was definitely the best option. The question was, who could I ask? Frankie and I came out of the alleyway and into Chestnut Close and I looked over at number nine. There was only person who might be able to help me with this mission.
Matthew.

CHAPTER 19

The next morning, I texted Matthew.

Hi, Matthew. Walk to school together? Melody x

I wasn't sure I'd get a reply but this time, I only had to wait five minutes.

Sure. M

We both came out of our houses at the same time and met at the end of my driveway. Matthew looked anxious, I thought. We started walking to school.

"How did your session go with Dr Rhodes yesterday?" I said.

Matthew took a deep breath. "It was terrible," he said. "I had to touch a bin lid with my bare hand. I thought my heart was going to explode, it was going so fast."

"And *did* you do it?" I said. "Did you manage to touch the bin?"

Matthew nodded. "Yes, I did it. It took me a while, though."

"Well then I wouldn't call that terrible," I said. "You did it, Matthew! You touched the bin! That's amazing."

Matthew laughed. "That's what Dr Rhodes said," he said.

We got to the high street and followed the crowd of students heading towards the school.

"What's going on with your house, then?" he said. "I can't believe you're moving."

"I know. It's horrible," I said. "Mum's at home this morning as we've got three more viewers."

"But why do you have to move anyway?"

"Mum said that we can't afford to stay here any longer. I've told her to talk to Dad. He might be able to help if he knew."

Matthew's eyes widened. He didn't know

anything about my dad. He'd never asked.

"Do you think she will?" he said.

I shrugged.

"She doesn't want to. I don't think she wants anything to do with him. But we only need him to help us out for a bit and then he can disappear again."

It was nice, just walking and chatting. It had been ages since we'd done that.

"Matthew, do you think you'd be able to do me a favour?" I said.

"Um. Maybe," said Matthew. He already looked worried and I hadn't even told him what it was yet.

"I need to get something from Mr Charles's house," I said.

"Why?" he said.

"That's the thing," I said. "I can't say why. All I *can* say is that it's very, very important."

Suddenly, there was a skidding noise behind us and some tiny stones hit the back of my legs.

"Ouch!" I said. I turned around. It was Jake. I let out a groan.

"What's very important?" he said.

"Jake. This is a private conversation!" I said.

"Melody was just asking for my help, but she

can't say why," Matthew said. I glared at him.

"Help with what?" said Jake. They both waited for an answer.

"With a matter of deception," I said.

Jake grinned, jumped off his bike and began walking beside us. "That sounds interesting," he said. He seemed much more cheerful than he had yesterday after rounders.

"I need to get something from Mr Charles's house without him knowing," I said. "And I need someone to help me do it."

"OK. And what are you getting?" said Jake.

"Yeah, you've at least got to tell us what it is!" said Matthew.

I gripped the strap of my school bag hard. I had to be really careful here.

"I can't," I said. "You've just got to trust me. There is a really important reason. It's a matter of life and death." I stopped. I'd already said too much.

"What!" said Matthew. "That's ridiculous, Melody. No way."

I waited for Jake to say something similar, but he didn't. "What exactly do you need us to do?" he said instead.

"After school I'm going to knock at Mr Charles's

house and pretend I've just popped round so that Teddy can see Frankie."

"OK. And where do we come in?" said Jake.

"*We*?" said Matthew.

"You need to be in Matthew's back garden," I said. "I need you to create a diversion to get Mr Charles, Teddy and Casey outside. Once they're out, keep them distracted for as long as you can while I try and find ... what I need to find."

Matthew didn't look very happy but Jake was grinning. "I've got an idea of what we could do!" he said. "Don't worry, Melody. Jake is on the case! See ya later!"

He sped off on his bike, leaving a cloud of dust behind him.

"Sorry, Melody. If you can't tell me anything else about it then I won't do it," said Matthew.

I stopped and turned to face him.

"Do you know what, Matthew?" I said. "Would it really hurt you to help me out for once in your life? You're meant to be my friend but Jake is being a better friend than you are. At least Jake says what he thinks to my face and not behind my back!"

Matthew looked like I'd slapped him.

"What do you mean?" he said.

"Jake told me you thought I was 'exhausting'," I said. "Remember now?"

I half hoped that Jake had made it up, but seeing Matthew's face turn a deep shade of pink told me that it was true. I stormed off.

Matthew found me at lunchtime, sitting on my own on the little mound of grass behind the computer block.

"Hi," he said.

"Hi," I said, not looking up at him. I saw his feet moving left and right. He was nervous.

"So, I've been thinking about what you said," he said. "I didn't mean to call you exhausting, Melody. Me and Jake were messing around and it just kind of came out. I'm sorry."

I kept my eyes down. He sat down on the grass beside me.

"I'll never forget how you stood by me last year when everyone else thought I was acting weird," he said. "I don't want to see you get into trouble. What are you getting from Mr Charles's house? Is it to do with you not wanting to move?" I shook my head. "OK then . . . is it something to do with your dad?"

"No. It's nothing to do with him. I'm just helping a

friend," I said. "He needs somewhere to stay for a bit."

Matthew frowned. "And you think he can stay at Mr Charles's house?" he said. Then his mouth fell open. "Hang on a minute! You think he can stay at number one! You're trying to get the key!"

I sighed. Everyone knew that Mr Charles had the key. He'd guessed it straight away. "Yes. But I can't tell you any more than that, OK? It's really, really important that this is kept just between us. You can't even tell Jake."

Matthew didn't look too happy, but he nodded. "I think Jake has got enough on his mind anyway," he said. "Mr Jenkins caught him running in the corridor and now he's got to spend every breaktime for a week clearing out the sports cupboard."

That punishment was way beyond the crime. For anyone else, running in the corridor just meant a negative mark against your name.

"He needs to tell somebody," I said. "He's being bullied by a teacher!"

"I know," said Matthew. "I said he should talk to his parents but he refuses."

The bell went for the end of lunch and I stood and picked up my bag. We began to walk to class.

"So, will you help me?" I said.

Matthew sighed.

"OK," he said. "I'll help you." He gave me a little smile. "Things are definitely never boring with you around, Melody."

On the way home from school, Matthew, Jake and I set out the plan.

"You two need to be ready in Matthew's garden," I said. "I'll go over to Mr Charles's house at 4.30 p.m. with Frankie. At approximately 4.35 p.m. I want you to make a distraction of some kind. Something that will get Mr Charles, Casey and Teddy outside to see what's going on. Then you need to keep them out there for as long as possible."

"No problem at all!" said Jake, grinning.

"How are we going to do that, though?" Matthew said. Jake patted him on the shoulder and Matthew flinched. He didn't like being touched.

"Don't you worry, Matty-boy. I told you, I've got an idea," he said. "I'll see ya later." He threw a leg over his bike, bumped down on to the road and sped off.

When I got home, I saw that Mum had left a note saying she'd gone to the supermarket to pick up a few things. I expect she'd noticed that most of the cheese had gone.

I looked at the clock. 3.45 p.m. I just had enough time to take Hal some food. I put a few things in a bag, including some flapjacks that Mum had brought home from the café.

I got Frankie and we hurried through the alley and into the graveyard, then made our way to the plague house.

"Hal! I've brought you some food. I've got to be quick because..."

I stopped. Hal was curled up on his blanket.

"Hal?" I said. "Are you asleep?"

There wasn't an answer.

"Hal?" I said.

Very slowly, I walked over. At first, I thought something terrible had happened and maybe Martin Stone had found him. Relief washed over me when I saw Hal's back rise and fall with his breaths.

I peered over his shoulder. His eyes were wide open and he was just staring at the dirty brick wall. He was wearing the black watch on one wrist and cradling it with his other hand.

"Hal? What's the matter? Are you ill?" I said.

Frankie sniffed his back and nudged him with

his nose. But Hal didn't move.

I let go of Frankie's lead and sat down beside him on the blanket and felt his hand. It was icy cold. I pulled the other blanket over him and took out a carton of juice from my bag, piercing the hole with the straw.

"Here, drink this," I said. I prodded the straw against his lips. He blinked a few times but continued to stare at nothing. I put the drink down.

"I've got you some more food," I said, trying to make my voice light. "Fruit, some cereal bars and oh, there's homemade flapjack too. *And* it's organic. I bet it will be the best flapjack you've ever tasted. Frankie, get your nose out!"

Hal blinked. Frankie could smell the food and he was snuffling his face into the bag.

"Frankie! That's Hal's food, not yours! Get off." I pulled on his collar but Frankie had managed to get hold of a cereal bar at the bottom of the bag. He snatched it with his front teeth and ran to the corner of the room.

"No! Frankie! Give it back, you silly dog! It's still got the wrapper on." I ran over and cornered him. His dark brown eyes twinkled at me as he held the cereal bar in his mouth, like a juicy bone. His tail was wagging madly.

"It's not a game! Drop it! Drop it now!" I said. I heard movement behind. Hal was sitting up, watching.

Frankie saw that my attention was elsewhere and suddenly darted to one side. I dived towards him, grabbing his collar. He dropped the cereal bar on to the floor and I picked it up by the corner of the packet. It was dripping with stringy saliva.

"I don't think you'll want this one any more," I said, turning back to Hal.

"How's it going with getting that key?" he said. His voice was like a whisper.

"I've got a plan to get it right now. I just wanted to bring you something to eat first," I said. I sat down and took out a square of flapjack. "Here, this might make you feel a bit better," I said.

Hal took the flapjack and stared at it in his hand. He took a tiny bite and then another.

"Hal?" I said. "Are you OK?"

He stopped eating but didn't look up. Then he shook his head slowly.

"I think I'm in trouble," he said. "I think ... I think I've been abandoned."

"What do you mean?" I said. "Abandoned by who?"

"My team," he said. "They still haven't made

contact. I think I'm on my own."

"But MI8 wouldn't let you down!" I said. "I'm sure they're working around the clock to get everything back online. They'll have it all up and running in no time, you'll see!"

Hal shook his head. A terrible thought occurred to me and I gasped.

"You don't think ... MI8 are *using* you? As bait?" I said.

Hal looked up at me, frowning. "Bait?" he said. His voice was still very quiet. "What do you mean?"

"I mean, maybe they stopped contact with you on purpose. Maybe they *want* you to stay here to try and lure Martin Stone in!"

He thought about it for a second. "I don't know what's going on any more," he said. "I'm so tired, Melody Bird."

I felt a tightness in my throat. I put my hand on his shoulder and squeezed.

"We'll get you into the house and everything will be better. OK?" I said. "I'm going to go and get that key right now."

I stood up and Hal smiled at me.

"Thank you," he said.

I was just about to go when I spotted a folded

piece of paper on the blanket next to him.

"Have you found another clue?" I said. I bent down and picked it up.

Again, the note was written in swirly, pencilled letters on creamy coloured paper. I began to read.

We have no flesh, feather or bone, yet we still have fingers and thumbs of our own.

"That's a weird one. *No flesh, feather or bone.* Do you have any ideas about what that means?" I said.

"No, not yet," he said. "I'll put it back now you've seen it." He hesitated. "I've just realized something. While I'm in the safe house, it will be down to you to check for more messages. Do you think you can do that, Melody Bird?"

I looked at him, then passed the folded riddle back.

"Of course, I can," I said. "I'm part of the team, aren't I?"

CHAPTER 20

I got to Mr Charles's house at 4.32 p.m., two minutes behind schedule. I rang the doorbell. Frankie sniffed at a brushed mat on the step that read WELCOME in big black letters.

"Ah! Melody," said Mr Charles, opening the door. He was wearing a red-checked shirt with the sleeves rolled up. "What can I do for you?"

"Hello, Mr Charles," I said, giving him my best, brilliant smile. Inside, my heart was hammering like a drum. Already I felt like he'd be able to tell I was up to something. "I was just taking Frankie for his walk and I wondered if Teddy would like to see him again?"

Teddy must have heard his name as he came thundering down the hallway.

"Doggy!" he said, diving on to his knees on the doormat. He grabbed Frankie's ears, one in each hand.

"Be careful," I said as Frankie yelped and pulled back. "You have to be really gentle. Here, I'll show you."

I crouched down and showed Teddy how to stroke Frankie's ears gently, the way he liked it. Teddy watched carefully, his big blue eyes wide. Then he reached out and softly stroked Frankie's ears.

"That's very kind of you, Melody," said Mr Charles. "Isn't it, Teddy?"

I waited to be asked in, but he just stood there. This wasn't part of the plan! I had to get inside! I decided to take matters into my own hands.

"I bet Casey would like to see Frankie as well," I said. "Why don't I come and check?"

Before Mr Charles had a chance to answer, I stepped into the house.

"Doggy's inside!" screeched Teddy in delight, thumping his socked feet up and down on the hallway carpet. I let Frankie lead me to the lounge.

Casey was sitting at a table in the corner, doing a jigsaw. The picture on the box was of a lion.

"Hello, Casey," I said. "Did you want to say hello to Frankie?"

She looked at Frankie and then at me.

"No," she said, returning to her puzzle. She really was a bit scary.

Teddy sat on the floor and Frankie laid down next to him. He smacked his lips together then yawned.

"Doggy is funny!" said Teddy. He began to stroke him from the top of his head right down to the end of his tail.

I glanced at a clock on the mantlepiece. It was 4.36 p.m. Matthew and Jake would make the distraction any second now. When they did, I would have to search fast. I'd start in the hallway. That seemed like the most likely place to put a key. That's where we put ours, anyway.

"I saw you had a few more viewings on the house today, Melody," said Mr Charles, sitting down in his armchair. "Has anyone made an offer to buy it yet?"

"No," I said. "We're not moving after all. Dad is going to help us out."

I felt myself flush slightly as I told the lie.

"Oh right," said Mr Charles. "I wondered whether he might have got in touch."

"Why would you wonder that?" I asked.

Mr Charles shrugged. "No reason."

That was an odd thing for him to say. Mr Charles would have known Dad when he was living with us, but why would he wonder if he had been in touch? After he left, Mum just told the neighbours that he had moved out and didn't tell anyone the extent of Dad's lies. That was just between us.

I watched Teddy stroking Frankie. 4.38 p.m., Matthew and Jake should have created the distraction by now. I was just thinking they must have failed in their mission, when there was an almighty crash outside.

Mr Charles leapt out of his seat.

"My greenhouse!" he said, rushing to the patio door that opened out on to the garden. What on earth had they done?!

Mr Charles yanked the door open.

"What is going on out here!" he yelled. Jake's head appeared over Matthew's garden fence.

"Sorry," he said. "We were playing football and—"

Mr Charles rushed out and Teddy followed, leaving Frankie snoring on the floor. For a moment,

I thought Casey wasn't going to go, but then she pushed her chair away and followed them out into the garden. It had worked! I had the house to myself! But for how long?

I ran to the hallway and looked on the side table that was beside the front door. There was a phone, an address book, a note pad and a couple of library books. I pulled open the little drawer. There was a box of tissues, some car keys and some pens, but no house keys. I looked around the front door to see if there were any key hooks but there weren't.

I hurried into the kitchen. On one side was a pile of post and some containers with TEA, COFFEE and COOKIES written on the front. I glanced out of the window at the garden. Mr Charles was standing in the middle of the lawn holding Teddy's hand and Jake and Matthew were both peering over the fence now. Mr Charles was gesturing at his brand-new greenhouse. One of the panes of glass was smashed and there was a football lying on the grass. I groaned. Did Jake have to go that far? I couldn't worry about that now. I had a mission to complete.

I spotted a ceramic dish next to a plant on the windowsill. In the dish were some paperclips, drawing pins, elastic bands and three light bulbs. There was also a key. It had a little red plastic fob attached to it with a label. On the label in pen was the number one.

I'd found it! I quickly slipped it into my school blazer pocket.

"What are you doing?" said a voice.

I gasped and span round.

"Oh, Casey! You made me jump. Did you want to see Frankie now?" I headed towards the door but she took a sidestep and blocked my way.

"I asked you what you were doing," she said. Her eyes darted around the kitchen, trying to work out what I'd been up to.

"I was just ... getting a drink of water," I said. She looked past me towards the sink.

"Where's the glass then?" she said. She narrowed her eyes.

"I put it away," I said. "Come on, let's go back to the lounge."

"You were looking for the letter, weren't you?" she said. There was a tiny smile on her lips.

"What letter?" I said.

"The letter Grandad got. He wasn't sure if he should tell you about it."

"What? What do you mean?" I said.

Casey smiled and raised her eyebrows.

"It was a letter to Grandad about you. He opened it and then talked about it. He does that a lot. He says his thoughts out loud and doesn't think anyone is listening. But I was."

I had a sick feeling in the pit of my stomach.

"Did he say who the letter was from?" I said.

Casey pressed her lips tightly together.

"Casey! Who was the letter from?" I said, sharply.

"Your dad," she said. Her eyes darted to the pile of post on the side and then back at me. I dived for the letters and flicked through them.

"Melody? Are you still here?" called Mr Charles, coming in from the patio doors in the lounge.

My eyes skimmed through the post and then I spotted it. An envelope with an address written in Dad's handwriting: *Mr Charles, 11 Chestnut Close*. I folded it in half and stuffed it into my pocket.

"Ah, there you are," said Mr Charles coming into the kitchen. "Those boys, honestly. Although I never see Matthew in the garden usually. Do you think he's cured now? You know, of that ABC or whatever it's called."

"OCD. And no, he's not cured. It doesn't work

like that," I said.

I went back into the lounge and picked up Frankie's lead. "I should head off now," I said.

"It's a bit of luck I've got a spare pane of glass," said Mr Charles, following me in. "I guess there's not much harm done. See you soon, Melody."

Teddy gave Frankie a goodbye pat on the bottom. Casey stood behind him, a little smile on her face.

"Bye, Melody!" she called.

I opened the front door and quickly closed it behind me, hoping that she wouldn't give me away.

CHAPTER 21

As soon as I got home I unclipped Frankie's lead, kicked my shoes off and ran upstairs.

I sat on my bed and took the letter out of my pocket. I traced the words on the front of the envelope with my finger. That was Dad's writing, *right there*. I recognized the curve of his C's in Chestnut Close. I'd know that handwriting anywhere.

My heart pounded as I turned the envelope over. The flap was unstuck where Mr Charles had already opened it.

I took out the single sheet of paper and began to read.

Dear Mr Charles,

I do hope that you are keeping well and that all is good with you at number eleven.

I expect receiving a letter from me may come as quite a surprise. After all, we didn't really know each other very well. We didn't speak much, except for the occasional chat about the weather and your garden. I guess I was too busy with my own concerns to think about talking to my neighbours. I regret that. You always seemed like a kind man.

As you can imagine, that is not the only regret I have in my life. To say I have made a mess of things is probably an understatement. I don't want sympathy, but to ask a favour. I'm sure your first instinct will be to say no, but I would ask that you read the whole of my letter before you decide. I would be very grateful.

What I wanted to ask you is this ...

"Melody! Are you home?"

Mum was pounding up the stairs. I quickly shoved the letter into the envelope and pressed the seal closed. But before I could hide it under my pillow, Mum came into my room.

"There you are," she said, smiling. "What's that you've got?" She nodded to the envelope.

"It's, um, s-some post. For Mr Charles. It came to us by mistake," I stammered.

"I'm popping over there now, I'll give it to him," she said, picking up the envelope without looking at the front.

All the air seemed to rush out of my lungs.

"Why are you going round there?" I asked.

"I just wanted to let him know that the café is donating some refreshments for the Big Graveyard Clear-Up on Saturday," she said.

I stared at the letter in her hand. What was it that Dad had asked? I *had* to know. I opened my mouth to offer to go with her or to take it there myself, but quickly shut it again. She might get suspicious and look more closely at the address. She would recognize Dad's handwriting, just like I had. If she knew it was from him I'd never get to read it. She'd probably just rip it up like she had done with his other letters!

"Could you set the table for dinner?" she said. "We've got a quiche and salad tonight. And can you tidy your room a bit? We've got some people coming for a second viewing tomorrow. The estate agent thinks they're really keen."

I couldn't speak due to the huge lump blocking my throat. Mum went downstairs with the letter in her hand. I glanced around my room. It didn't look like it needed tidying to me, but I quickly picked up some dirty socks and straightened the quilt on my bed. That would do. I heard the front door shut and I ran downstairs to the lounge and peeked around the curtain. Mr Charles was just answering the door to Mum. Would he recognize the letter and realize it had been stolen? I held my breath. They appeared to be talking about something and then Mum gave him the envelope. Teddy appeared and Mr Charles gave him the letter without looking at it. He said something to him and Teddy toddled off towards the kitchen. I breathed out again.

I quickly laid the table like Mum had asked, then I put my trainers on and sprinted to the plague house.

When I got there, Hal was standing, looking out of the window.

"Melody Bird!" he said, spinning round.

"I got the key," I said. "Tomorrow is Wednesday

and I think we should move you then. That means you'll be well out of the way before the clear-up on Saturday."

Hal smiled. "I knew you'd do it," he said.

I turned to go.

"Are you OK?" he said. "You look a bit shaken up. Did something go wrong?"

I shook my head. "I'm fine," I said.

Hal took a step towards me.

"Do you want to talk about it?" he said.

For a moment, I considered telling him about Dad's letter. About what happened after our trip to the circus when Dad left us for good. About the lies and how Mum was so shell-shocked she couldn't eat for three days. But just thinking about it made a lump form in my throat. I couldn't get the words out.

"Everything is fine," I said. To change the subject, I continued, "Have you managed to solve the riddle?"

"*We have no flesh, feather or bone, yet we still have fingers and thumbs of our own,*" said Hal. "I haven't figured it out yet, but I'll keep trying."

My head felt too tired to think.

"I'd better get home now," I said. "I'll see you tomorrow, Hal."

Hal looked at me with a worried expression on his face. I turned and walked away.

The words from Dad's letter were still floating around my mind when I walked along the graveyard path. I kept trying to remember what they said, but I couldn't quite grasp hold of them. I could only think of the last part I'd read. *What I wanted to ask you is this . . .*

What was it that he'd asked Mr Charles?

When I got to Chestnut Close I looked over at number eleven. Behind that door was Dad's letter. And somehow, I had to get it back.

CHAPTER 22

The key to number one Chestnut Close was still in my blazer pocket when I walked to school the next morning. When Mum came back from returning the letter to Mr Charles's house, she didn't say anything, so my suspicions were correct. Neither of them had looked closely enough to realize who it was from. Hopefully, Teddy had just put it with all of the other post on the kitchen counter and Mr Charles would have been none the wiser. I was safe.

I couldn't do anything about the letter while I was at school, so I decided to push it out of my mind for now and focus on the next riddle.

Matthew sat beside me in my first class, which

was French. At the start of our lesson, Miss Kent told us to talk to the person beside us in French about our hobbies. Instead, Matthew took the chance to question me.

"You got the key, then?" he said.

"Yes," I said. "Smashing a football into a greenhouse was a bit extreme, don't you think? Typical Jake."

"He was aiming for the fishpond, actually," said Matthew. "Mr Charles loves those fish and he thought if he heard a splash he'd run out."

I glanced at him. He was smiling. He must have found it quite fun in the end.

"Who is it you're going to sneak into number one?" he asked.

Miss Kent walked past and Matthew started to speak French. He was saying something about how much he liked football, even though I knew he didn't play. As soon as our teacher moved on, he went back to English.

"You can trust me, you know," he said.

If there was one person I could trust in the whole wide world it was Matthew Corbin. We'd been through quite a lot together last summer. He *was* my best friend after all. Even if things had been weird between us lately.

"OK. But you must swear not to tell anyone. Not your parents. Not Jake. No one," I said.

Matthew nodded. "I won't tell a soul," he said.

I took a deep breath.

"There's someone hiding in the graveyard," I said. "He's in trouble and I've said he can stay at number one until he can get help."

Matthew's eyes widened. I could tell this wasn't what he was expecting at all.

"What do you mean, there's someone hiding in the graveyard?" he said. "Who is he?"

"A boy called Hal," I said.

Matthew checked around for Miss Kent but she was at the back of the class.

"Don't his parents know where he is?" he said. "How old is he?"

"I don't know. Fifteen? Maybe sixteen?"

"He must have run away," said Matthew.

"No! It's nothing like that," I said. "He's doing some work for a secret agency. But the plans that were in place have gone a bit ... wrong. And there's going to be a clean-up in the graveyard on Saturday, so he needs somewhere to stay for a few days."

Saying it out loud made it all sound so unbelievable.

"A secret agency? Seriously?!" Matthew said. There was a laugh in his voice. "How do you know he's not lying? He could be a murderer! Or a thief on the run. A wanted criminal!"

"He's not!" I snapped. "He's helping to catch those kinds of people! Oh, I *knew* I shouldn't have told you. Just forget I said anything, OK?"

We sat in silence for the rest of the lesson, apart from practising a few French phrases on each other. Fortunately, it was the only one I had all day with Matthew so he didn't get a chance to question me again. I was so annoyed with myself for telling him. I had promised Hal I wouldn't. And now I'd risked *everything*!

My last lesson of the day was maths. Matthew was in the top set and I was in the middle set, along with Jake. Our maths teacher, Mrs Bryant, was off sick so we were waiting to see who was going to appear as a stand-in.

Everyone seemed to think that this was a good reason to mess around. The whole class were chatting and, apart from a couple of us, hardly anyone was sitting at their desks. Someone threw a pencil case across the room which hit a boy called Daniel on the shoulder. Daniel grabbed a bright yellow highlighter pen from his desk and chucked it back across the room. Soon everyone was throwing things. Rolled-up sheets of paper, rulers and pencils flew over our heads.

I stayed in my seat, happy to be out of it. I hated it when everyone behaved like this. I got my maths book and opened it to a new page and put my head down. Just then, the door swung open and we saw who our stand-in teacher was going to be.

It was Mr Jenkins.

There was a mad scramble as everyone rushed back to their seats. Mr Jenkins wasn't a teacher to be messed with. But someone couldn't have seen he was there, because a bright green eraser soared across the room and smacked Mr Jenkins right on the side of his nose.

Mr Jenkins flinched as it hit him, then stood dead still. The green eraser fell to the floor, bounced once, twice, then came to a rest beside his trainer. He bent down and picked it up.

"Who threw this?" he said. He held the eraser between his thumb and index finger, as if he were holding up an emerald into the light.

Nobody said a word.

"Maybe you didn't hear me," said Mr Jenkins with a nasty smile. "I said, WHO. THREW. THIS?"

Everyone jumped as he shouted. Mr Jenkins had the ability to go from a whisper to eardrum-shattering loudness within seconds. Again, no one spoke.

"Walking into this classroom right now was like walking into a chimpanzee enclosure at the ZOO!" Mr Jenkins bellowed. He slowly paced around the room. "Now, I'm going to ask for a final time. Who threw this?"

The room was utterly silent. Mr Jenkins came to a stop beside Jake's desk which was in the corner, on the other side of the classroom from me. My heart sank.

"Jake Bishop," said Mr Jenkins. "Was it you? Did you throw the eraser?"

I didn't want to look to see Jake's pale face, not meeting Mr Jenkins's gaze.

"No, Sir," he said, quietly.

Mr Jenkins walked back down the aisle to the front of the room.

"I find that hard to believe," he said. "Given that you're usually the centre of any disturbance. Did anyone see Jake Bishop throw it? Anyone?" No one said a thing. "Come on, someone must have seen him!"

He wanted it to be Jake but he couldn't prove it. From the angle that the eraser had been travelling across the room, there was no way Jake could have thrown it. Silence. I saw Mr Jenkins shrug slightly. He was going to have to leave it, I thought. But then I heard Jake's chair scrape as he stood up.

"It wasn't me, all right? Trying to pin the blame on to me won't work. Not this time!"

I twisted round. Jake was standing with his clenched hands by his sides. He was breathing fast. I looked back at Mr Jenkins and noticed the corners of his mouth turning up slightly. This was *exactly* what he wanted.

A reaction.

"Sit down, Jake. You're making a fool of yourself," he said.

I shut my eyes and silently begged for Jake to sit back down, but he didn't.

"Last chance, Bishop. Or else it's a month of detentions. *Did you throw the eraser?*" Jake stayed silent.

I felt so sorry for Jake. OK, so he could be utterly

horrible sometimes, but he didn't deserve this. Mr Jenkins was being completely unjust. And if there was anything I didn't like, it was seeing someone treated unfairly. Even *if* it was Jake Bishop.

I found myself slowly pushing my chair back. It made a terrible screeching sound and every single face turned around to see what I was doing. I stood up. My knees trembled and my heart pounded. Mr Jenkins stared at me, his mouth slightly parted.

"I threw the eraser!" I said loudly.

There was a gasp around the room.

Mr Jenkins took a step closer, frowning.

"What did you say?" he said.

I swallowed.

"I threw the eraser," I said, a little quieter this time. I'd never been faced with Mr Jenkins's anger before. It felt like his eyes were penetrating into my brain. This had been a terrible mistake.

Just then, there was the sound of another chair being scraped backwards. A few rows in front I could see Daniel, the boy who owned the rubber, slowly rise to his feet.

"I threw the eraser!" he said, loudly.

Mr Jenkins head shot round.

"You?" he said.

Someone else stood up. This time it was Samira in the very front row. Samira was the best student in our year.

"I threw the eraser!" she yelled.

Mr Jenkins spun round, but then Helena stood up. She looked around at everyone, her face bright red, and then I saw her take a deep breath. "I threw the eraser," she yelled.

Next was Thomas who jumped to his feet.

"I THREW THE ERASER!" he yelled, laughing loudly.

"I threw the eraser!"

"I THREW THE ERASER!"

I looked around, as student after student stood up. I looked at Jake as he realized what everyone was doing. He had some colour back in his cheeks. Soon every single child in the room was standing up at their desk, declaring that they had thrown the eraser.

We stood in silence, waiting for Mr Jenkins to say something. He looked at each of our faces in turn, until his eyes rested on one person: Jake.

"Jake Bishop," he said. "Get out."

There was a moment of quiet as Jake hesitated, then his chair crashed to the floor as he grabbed his bag and stormed through the classroom, slamming the door behind him.

Mr Jenkins walked to his desk. His back was to us and I saw it rise and fall as he took a very deep breath. After a few seconds, he turned to face us again.

"Who would like to update me on what you did in your last lesson?" he said.

We all looked at each other and then slowly began to sit back down. It was pointless. Mr Jenkins was never wrong. Even a class of thirty couldn't convince him otherwise.

CHAPTER 23

Matthew caught up with me when I was walking home.

"I heard about what happened in your maths class," he said. "That was a brave thing to do."

"I think I just ended up getting Jake into more trouble," I said. "Have you seen him? He walked out and didn't come back."

Matthew shook his head. "He probably went home," he said.

"He should definitely tell someone at school what's going on. Or his mum at least," I said. "He's not going to be able to solve this on his own."

"Yeah," said Matthew. "Just like you need to tell someone about this person in the graveyard."

I quickened my step. I'd walked right into that one. "Just forget I ever said anything, OK?" I said.

"But he could be dangerous!" said Matthew, hurrying to keep up with me. "Have you thought about that?"

I pictured Martin Stone and the gun hidden underneath his jacket. *He* was the dangerous one, not Hal.

"Can I come and meet him? At least then I can find out what he's like," said Matthew.

I laughed. "Last time I checked you weren't too keen to visit the plague house."

"Is that where he's been hiding?" said Matthew. He looked horrified.

""Yes. So you wouldn't be able to manage it, would you?" I said. I was being cruel but I needed to put him off the idea immediately, even if it meant upsetting him.

I glanced at him as we walked along. He was staring at the pavement and clearly thinking hard.

"You know what, Melody?" he said. "If it meant finding out more about Hal, then yes I would visit the plague house."

I felt a warm glow inside. He was willing to face his fears to help me. I was carrying so many secrets at the moment: Hal, my dad's letter, stealing the key to number one... Each one was like a heavy block, resting on my shoulders. If Matthew was involved, maybe that weight would lighten a little? It would be nice to not have all these worries on my own.

"OK," I said. "I have to get Hal some food but I can meet you there in a bit. Please, you must promise not to tell *anyone*."

I hadn't told him about Martin Stone or the gun yet. He had no idea how serious this was. He nodded.

"Head towards the top corner of the graveyard. The oldest part. There's a hole in a wall and the plague house is just beyond there," I said.

"I'll meet you there in twenty minutes," he said.

When I got home, Mum was still at work. I collected some food for Hal. I wondered how he'd react to Matthew showing up. Would he be angry with me? I pushed the thought out of my head. There was nothing I could do about it now.

Frankie sat and watched as I put crisps, yoghurt and fruit into a plastic bag. I had a feeling it wouldn't be long before Mum began to notice that food was going missing. I grabbed a little spoon from the drawer for the yoghurt.

"Come on, Frankie," I said. "Walkies."

Frankie climbed out of his bed and wagged his tail all the way to the front door.

Hal was waiting for me with a big smile.

"Hi!" he said, brightly. I noticed that all of his things in the room had been packed away. His rucksack was down by his feet.

"Hal? There's something I need to tell you," I said. I put the bag of food down. "It's really nothing to worry about as it's only Matthew. If you can trust anyone in the world, you can trust him." I laughed, but it was because I was nervous.

Hal's face dropped.

"What have you done, Melody?" he said. "You haven't told anyone I'm here, have you?"

"I had to," I said. "Matthew and Jake helped me to distract Mr Charles so that I could get the key. Matthew knows you're here, but you can trust him *entirely*!"

Hal walked around the room.

"I can't believe this," he said, shaking his head. "I thought you were a brilliant asset to the team, Melody Bird. You've betrayed my trust. Why?"

He stopped in front of me.

"I haven't!" I said. "You *can* trust me. I wouldn't have told Matthew if I thought it would put you in danger, I promise."

"Melody? Are you there?" called a voice. It was Matthew.

Frankie pulled on his lead to go and see. Hal looked even more alarmed.

"He's *here*?" he said to me, through gritted teeth.

"He's wanted to meet you for himself," I said. "He was worried about me. I didn't want him to tell his parents, so I said he could."

"*What?*" said Hal. "One minute you're telling me I can trust this Matthew, and the next you're saying he might tell someone!"

"Ah, there you are." Matthew walked sheepishly into the room. He was wearing a long coat zipped up at the front and his hands were stuffed into the pockets. I felt an ache in my heart. It must have taken so much courage for him to come here, into a *plague house*. Even though his logical brain would know that any danger of disease had long gone, his OCD brain would be trying to take over. Inside he'd be trying hard to ignore the feeling that there were germs crawling all over the walls.

"Hello," said Matthew. "I guess you must be Hal?"

Hal's eyes widened.

"It's you," he said.

Matthew looked taken aback. He looked at me and then at back at Hal.

"Do I know you?" he said.

Hal had backed up against the window ledge. He shook his head.

"No... Sorry. I was mistaken," he said.

Matthew frowned at me and then took a step closer. "Melody told me that you're in some kind of trouble? What's going on?" he said.

His voice was louder than usual and he was holding his head high. It was what he did when he was trying to be brave.

Hal folded his arms. I waited for him to explain why he was here, camping out in a plague house, but he was silent.

"Tell him about Martin Stone, Hal!" I said. "The mastermind criminal! And about MI8 and your team who might have double crossed you. And the gun!"

Matthew snorted. "A gun? MI8?" he said. He glanced at Hal. "Are you for real?"

Hal swallowed and stared at the floor. He looked really uncomfortable. And more worryingly, he didn't attempt to back me up.

"This is Secret Agent Hal Vincent," I said, firmly. "He's a spy working on an important mission to try and recover an extremely valuable necklace. He's been staying here because he has been staking out a criminal called Martin Stone, who has a gun. But now he's at risk of being found by Stone *and* we think his team might have double crossed him. They could be using him as bait. Also, he can't stay here much longer because on Saturday the graveyard is going to full of people clearing it up! *That's* why we need to get him to safety. That's why I took the key for number one."

Matthew began to laugh.

"I'm sorry, Melody, but are you *serious*? If *he's* a spy then Frankie is a tiger," he said. Frankie, who was sitting by Matthew's feet, wagged his tail.

"Who are you really?" said Matthew to Hal. "You're a thief, aren't you? Are you actually staking out the houses in the close?"

I thought back to when I'd spotted Hal looking at the houses through the binoculars. I never did ask what it was he'd been doing. Was he checking out access points to get into the houses?

Hal looked down at the ground. "Melody Bird is telling the truth," he said, quietly. "I'm a spy and I work for MI8."

Just then, there was the sound of footsteps crossing the floor in the other room. Frankie pulled on his lead again. I got ready to run, thinking Martin Stone or one of his gang had found us! But then the intruder spoke.

"Who's a spy?" said a voice, and Jake walked into the room. He must have followed us!

"What are *you* doing here?" I said.

"I could ask you the same thing!" he said. He looked at me, then Matthew and then Hal. His jaw dropped.

"Who are you?" he said. "And WHY ARE YOU WEARING MY CLOTHES?"

CHAPTER 24

Everything went a bit strange then.

"So, you've stolen my clothes," said Jake. "What else have you got, eh?"

He went to pick up Hal's rucksack, but Hal dived forward and grabbed it, clasping it close to his chest. Jake picked up the plastic bag filled with food instead and tipped it on to the floor. Frankie made a run for the food and I dropped his lead.

"Stop it, Jake! He hasn't been stealing! I brought him these," I said, trying to pick all the things up before Frankie got to them.

I grabbed Frankie's lead and pulled him away from the food.

"This is Hal," said Matthew. "*Apparently* he's a secret agent working for an organization called MI8. He's staking out someone called Martin Stone who has a gun." I could tell Matthew felt embarrassed for me and that made me feel even worse.

"A gun?" said Jake. "Really, Melody?"

I nodded. "Yes!" I said. "I saw it. This is serious, Jake!"

He shook his head. "Don't be stupid. There's no such thing as MI8," he said. "He's a fraud! And he stole my clothes!"

I moved to stand beside Hal. I noticed that his hands were trembling slightly.

"Jake, there are highly confidential things going on around us that we don't even realize. Top secret stuff. Stuff that is in our best interest *not* to know about." I tried to remember exactly how Hal had explained it to me when I'd first met him. "Hal didn't steal your clothes. *I* did," I said.

"You did?" said Jake.

I nodded. "He needed some clothes, so I took your hoodie and jeans from your washing line. The food in the bag is all from my cupboard," I said.

Jake glared at Hal. "Can't he speak for himself?" he said.

It *was* strange that Hal hadn't said a word. Especially as he would have been trained for situations like this.

"Hal? Tell them everything you told me. *Please*," I said.

"Yeah, come on then," said Jake. "What have you got to say for yourself, *Special Agent Hal*?"

Hal blinked a few times and stared at the ground. Even though he was standing right there it felt like he was slowly vanishing away in front of our eyes, like a strange magic trick.

"Right," said Jake. "You've got exactly five seconds to prove you're a secret agent, or I'm going to call the police." He took his mobile out of his pocket and unlocked the screen.

"Jake! No!" I said.

Hal began to breathe really fast, like he'd been running. His hands were clenched as he clutched his rucksack to his chest.

"OK. Hold on," he said. He frowned. "I can prove it."

"FIVE!" shouted Jake. He had his finger poised over the screen.

"Jake, stop it!" I said.

"FOUR!" said Jake.

Hal began to pace around the room, his brow furrowed.

"THREE! TWO!"

"Leave him be, Jake!" I said. Frankie began to bark excitedly.

"ONE!"

"OK!" shouted Hal. "I can prove it! All right?"

He cleared his throat and then took a deep breath.

"You're Jake Bishop," he said quietly. "You live with your mum at number five Chestnut Close. Your older brother lives in Australia. You really don't like your PE teacher, Mr Jenkins. In fact, I would go as far as to say that Mr Jenkins is emotionally bullying you. And you have allergies. Severe ones. They cause you to have skin flare-ups and because of this you were picked on in the past. You find it hard to trust people, so you tend to hurt them before they can hurt you."

Jake's eyes widened and he swallowed.

"That proves nothing," he said. "That's all stuff you've probably heard from Melody."

He looked at me and I nodded slowly. I *had* told Hal all of those things, apart from the bit about him not trusting people. Hal had worked that out for himself.

"You've got to do better than that!" said Jake. He held his phone up again, ready to dial 999.

Hal turned towards Matthew.

"You are Matthew Corbin. You are thirteen and the son of Sheila and Brian. You live at number nine Chestnut Close. You have a cat called Nigel who you are scared to touch because you think he has germs on him. You're frightened that germs will make you ill. You have a condition called Obsessive Compulsive Disorder."

Matthew shrugged. "And?" he said. "Knowing things about me doesn't make you a spy. Like Jake said, Melody probably told you all that."

Hal took another step closer.

"You visit a psychotherapist called Dr Rhodes every Monday. Your appointment is always at five p.m. Sometimes your mum or dad drop you off and sometimes you walk there. Occasionally you miss a session but, on the whole, you are a regular patient."

Matthew looked at me and blinked a few times. Hal carried on. "A few weeks ago, you came out of Dr Rhodes's office and waited for your dad to pick you up. He usually pulls into the bus lane and you jump in – not technically allowed, but not a serious crime. But this time, your dad was late," he said.

"Thirteen minutes late to be precise."

"Melody?" said Matthew to me. "What's going on?"

I shook my head. I had no idea. I hadn't known any of this.

"On that day there was a woman sitting with her son at the bus stop," said Hal. "They started talking to you. The boy was eating a bag of sweets and offered you one, but you refused. The boy and his mum got on the bus and you waited for six more minutes before your dad appeared."

"This is well creepy," said Jake. He put his phone down.

Matthew looked horrified. "Have you been following me?" he said.

"Matthew Corbin, last summer you were integral in solving a case concerning a missing child – Teddy Dawson. After the case was closed, you became of interest to MI8," said Hal. He had his fingertips pressed together as he walked around the room.

"What?!" said Matthew. "But I haven't done anything wrong!"

Hal laughed. "No, you misunderstand me. You are not a person of interest due to criminal behaviour, but because of your potential."

Matthew's eyes widened and his mouth fell open.

"You were followed by MI8 because you were the perfect candidate to join our team," said Hal. "As a spy."

CHAPTER 25

"What?" screeched Jake. "Matthew? A spy? Don't be ridiculous! Matthew couldn't be a spy!" He began to laugh as if this was the most outlandish thing he'd ever heard. I thought he sounded a bit jealous.

"All right, Jake," said Matthew. "You've made your point."

Matthew turned to Hal. "Let me get this right. You've been watching me ever since the Teddy Dawson case was cracked, assessing me to see whether I could join MI8?"

Hal nodded. "Correct," he said. "We have files on you, Matthew Corbin."

I noticed a flicker of a smile on Matthew's face. He was thrilled, I could tell.

"And what was the outcome?" I said.

Hal shrugged. "I would guess that the fact that you haven't been approached, Matthew, means that you were deemed unsuitable," he said. "My superiors make those kinds of decisions. I believe we stopped following you a few weeks back."

We were all silent, thinking about what Hal had just told us.

"Anyway, I hope that's enough proof for you," said Hal.

I noticed Jake still looked unconvinced, but Matthew looked impressed. And no wonder. Hal knew things about Matthew that even I didn't know!

"Not only is Hal a secret agent, but he can do magic as well!" I said. "Why don't you show them a trick?"

Hal shrugged.

"OK," he said. He unzipped the pocket of his rucksack and took out the smooth pebble that had been in the windowsill.

"Here we have a pebble, just a normal pebble," said Hal, turning into a magician before our very eyes. "As you can see, there is nothing strange about this pebble at all."

Hal smiled and held the pebble between his index finger and thumb then raised his other hand as he formed a fist around it. He shook his fist a few times, then unfurled both of his hands, revealing empty palms.

"Oh wow," said Matthew. "That's so cool!"

I giggled. Only Jake didn't look impressed.

"Right. Listen," I said. "We need to talk about more important things now. Hal is in danger. The Big Graveyard Clear-up is happening in three days. We need to get him to number one, where he can hide out for a while. It's going to be his safe house."

"Why doesn't he just go home?" said Jake. "Or make a phone call to MI8?"

"We have procedures to adhere to which are strictly confidential," Hal said coolly. "Besides, we are at a critical stage in the investigation."

"Hal is staking out a criminal called Martin Stone who has been communicating with his gang in the graveyard," I said. "*He's* the one with the gun. He was behind a jewellery theft in a museum in Cambridge."

Jake opened his mouth to interrupt.

"Before you ask, Jake, I looked it up," I said. "The Kingfisher Necklace was taken from the museum in Cambridge in 2015 and no trace of it was ever found."

Jake closed his mouth.

"We are getting closer to finding out where the necklace is hidden before it is passed on to its new owner," I went on. "When we've found it, we can make a move."

"We?" said Matthew. "Melody, are you involved in this too?"

I nodded.

"Melody has been instrumental in solving some of the messages being passed between the criminals," said Hal. "I couldn't have got this far without her input."

I felt a glow inside my stomach.

"What kind of messages?" said Jake.

"Messages left on a gravestone. They take the form of riddles and I believe that they will eventually lead to the whereabouts of the necklace. If we can solve them before Stone does, and locate the necklace, then it's game over for him," said Hal. He turned to me. "Have you had any luck with the latest message, Melody?"

"No, not yet," I said. I'd not given it much thought, what with getting the key and seeing my dad's letter. "Can I tell them about it?"

Hal nodded. I turned to Matthew.

"Matthew, you are going to *love* this," I said. "It says: '*We have no flesh, feather or bone, yet we still have fingers and thumbs of our own*'."

Matthew scrunched up his nose as he thought about it. "What about a fish?" he said. "No ... it can't be that. They don't have fingers."

"A monkey?" said Jake. "A dog? A goat?"

Matthew laughed. "They all have flesh and bones, silly!" he said. Jake looked hurt.

"And it can't be a bird as they have flesh, bones *and* feathers," I said. "What about a reptile? Or an insect?"

Matthew took a hand out of his pocket to scratch his head. My heart sank. He was wearing gloves, the plastic ones he used to wear when his OCD was at its worst last year. Coming to the plague house must have caused him such anxiety that he'd felt the need to wear them again, to protect him from germs. He had taken a step backwards and it was all my fault.

"Oh, Matthew," I said, looking at his hands. "I'm so sorry. You shouldn't have come here."

But Matthew was staring at his hand.

"Hang on. I've got it!" he said. "The answer to the riddle!"

"You've solved it already?! I knew it!" I said.

He grinned at me.

"It's not an animal at all! Think of something else. Something not living," he said.

I wracked my brain. No flesh. No feathers. But it had fingers and a thumb. Now that I knew it wasn't alive, it suddenly made complete sense. Matthew had the answer right in his pockets.

"It's gloves!" I shouted. "Of course! That's brilliant."

Matthew was still grinning at me. I *knew* he'd like the riddles.

"But that's just stupid," said Jake. "Why would some dangerous criminals make up rubbish like that?"

"It's not stupid!" I said. "We're building up a pattern here. So far, all the clues have led to objects. A mirror, an anchor and now the gloves. We just need to work out what they mean when we put them together."

"I get what Jake is saying, though," said Matthew. "It's all a bit weird, don't you think?

Serious criminals, leaving each other handwritten notes that basically anyone could find?"

Hal smiled. "People expect there to be more high-tech methods in the criminal underworld, but you'd be surprised. Sometimes it is just as basic as passing notes," he said. "In fact, I intercepted another message from the gravestone today."

Jake leapt forward and snatched the slip of paper.

"*Bright like diamonds, hard like rock, I'm crushed or cubed or solid block*," he read.

"Really? That's so easy!" said Matthew.

"Hang on. Don't tell me," said Jake, rereading the riddle. His lips moved silently. I'd also worked it out. It wasn't as hard as the other ones. The word "cubed" gave it away.

"Glass?" said Jake, looking up.

"No, it's ice," said Matthew. "It's bright like diamonds but hard and it can be crushed or cubed in drink. Or a solid block."

"This is a load of rubbish," said Jake. "You've both lost your minds if you believe this is real!" He walked across the room to the door and waited.

"Matthew? Are you coming?" said Jake. Matthew didn't move.

"Not right now. I'll head back in a bit," he said.

"Fine. You two stay here and play imaginary games. I've had enough of this. I've got some planning of my own to do. See you later, losers!" Jake stormed out of the cottage.

"You don't think he'll tell anyone, do you?" I said to Matthew.

"No. He's not a grass," he said. "He'll get over it."

"I think I should relocate to the safe house now," said Hal. I'd forgotten about that.

"Wouldn't it be better to go later?" said Matthew. "There are far too many people around. I just saw Hannah on the way here."

"You're right," I said. I turned to Hal. "We'll come back. After dark. Let's say . . . midnight?"

I looked at Matthew. He was a part of this now. One of the team.

"Matthew, will you come too?" I said.

Matthew looked at me, and then at Hal.

"Sure," he said.

CHAPTER 26

Getting out of my house had been surprisingly easy. Mum's bedroom light had turned off just before eleven and I could hear her soft snores about ten minutes later. I had been worried that Frankie might make a noise, but he didn't even lift his head when I slipped out of the front door.

I was meeting Matthew by the alley. He eventually appeared at ten past twelve. He hurried over to me, his face pale in the moonlight.

"You're late!" I whispered.

"I know. Dad's only just gone to bed so I had to make sure he was asleep! Ready?" he said.

"Ready!" I grinned.

I'd never been in the graveyard at night. It almost felt like a different place. The daylight colours of greens, yellows and greys had been replaced with the night-time shades of deep purples, blacks and browns. It was still beautiful.

We headed past the horse chestnut tree and something screeched. Matthew jumped.

"What was that?" he said.

"Just a fox," I said.

He took a deep breath and sped up. "Come on. Let's get this over with," he said. I think the excitement of being considered "spy-material" might have been wearing off.

"Thanks for coming, Matthew," I said. "It's nice having you here. It was getting hard not being able to talk about what was going on."

"I couldn't let you go on your own, could I?" said Matthew.

When we got to the plague house, Hal was waiting outside, sitting up against the wall.

"You're here!" he said, jumping up. "I wasn't sure of the time, so I just thought I'd wait out here for you. I've been looking at the moon. Isn't it beautiful?"

Matthew and I both turned to look up at the bright, silver orb in the sky.

"Wow. It's so bright," said Matthew. It really was stunning.

Hal swung his rucksack on to his shoulder and picked up the two rolled-up blankets, tucking them under his arm.

"Ready?" he said.

"Yep!" I said. "Let's go."

"Remember, Melody, you'll have to check for messages now," said Hal.

"Of course!" I said. How exciting was this!

As we walked through the graveyard, Matthew kept checking behind us every few steps. I wasn't sure if he was looking for ghosts or dangerous criminals, but he was certainly very jumpy.

"There's no one there, Matthew," I said. "Just relax." He nodded but I could see he was scared. I decided talking normally might help.

"What did you get up to this evening?" I said. "Anything good?" We were nearly at the alleyway.

"Not much. I watched a bit of YouTube," he whispered. Our feet crunched on the stones of the alleyway as we headed to Chestnut Close. The streetlights made it feel less dark. "Then we had dinner. Then I did homework."

"What's YouTube?" Hal asked.

Matthew went to laugh, then realized Hal was being serious. "You don't know what YouTube is?" he said, quietly.

Just then I spotted someone and gasped.

"Look! It's Old Nina," I said. She placed two empty milk bottles on to her doorstep, then stopped to look up at the moon. We were just about to step back into the shadows when she turned around and saw us. She made her way down to her garden gate and folded her arms, waiting for us to come over.

"Leave the talking to me," I said, under my breath.

She was wearing a pale-yellow jumper with her blue brooch pinned to one side. As we approached her, she looked at the three of us in turn.

"Hello, Melody. Matthew," she said. Her eyes rested on Hal. "What on earth are you doing out at this hour?"

"We're doing a science project," I said. "We had to do, um, a night-time safari. Spotting nocturnal wildlife and that."

Hal was staring at Old Nina's home, The Rectory. "I really like your house. It looks like a vampire could live there!" he said. He came and stood next to her, looking up at the house.

"I guess it *is* a little spooky," said Old Nina. "But

it's home to me. Are you a friend of Melody and Matthew's?"

I nodded. "Yes. He's in our science class. He's staying over at mine. Aren't you, Hal?"

I saw Hal flinch when I said his name out loud. I'd given it away instantly! But Old Nina nodded. "I don't know. These school projects they come up with nowadays. Night safaris!" she said. "It was nice to see you all."

She headed back up the path. We walked on a bit and waited for the door to close behind her.

"OK. Let's go," I said.

The three of us crossed the road towards number one. I took the key out of my pocket and fumbled it into the lock. The door opened and we all piled into the hallway. I quickly shut the door behind us and put the key back in my pocket. Matthew went to switch on the light.

"No!" I said. "No lights. There can't be any sign that anyone is in here."

Hal dropped his blankets and rucksack on to the floor as he looked around. The house smelled musty and stale, like the air had been left inside for too long. The hallway had a deep, pink-coloured carpet and floral wallpaper.

"This place is incredible," said Hal. Matthew and I looked at each other. Hal ran to the lounge, then his head reappeared around the door.

"Guys! There's a *MASSIVE TELEVISION* in here!" he shouted.

"Shhhh!" I said. "My mum is just next door! If she hears you it's over. You can't put the TV on and you must stay away from the windows in case you are seen."

Hal nodded. He ran to the dining room and then through into the kitchen. We followed him.

"Look at the fridge!" he said, quieter this time. "It's HUGE!" He opened and closed it a few times, making the light turn on and off. There were a few jars of pickles on one of the shelves but not much else. I didn't understand why he seemed so excited. It was just a normal fridge.

"It's not that big," said Matthew. "It's half the size of our one, actually."

Hal giggled. "Don't be silly!" he said. Matthew frowned at me as if to say *"what's going on?"* but I had no idea. Why was Hal suddenly acting so weird? Maybe it was just the relief of getting here. The fear of being abandoned by MI8 and discovered by Martin Stone must have been very stressful.

"Are you all right?" said Matthew.

Hal started giggling.

"I'm fine! This place is brilliant!" he said. "Thank you."

He was like an excitable toddler. He suddenly rushed off to the lounge. Matthew and I looked at each other, then followed him. Hal was sprawled out on the squishy sofa. He had his arms folded behind his head and his ankles were crossed on a cushion.

"You know what? I think I'm going to like it here," he said with a grin.

When I went to bed later, I listened for any noises coming from next door. I was worried that Hal might turn the TV on or thump up and down the stairs. If Mum heard anything, she'd tell Mr Charles. Hal would be found and everything would be over. But, as much as my ears were straining to hear any sign of life, all was quiet. As far as everyone else was concerned, number one was still empty.

That night I had a bad dream. It was about Dad. I never usually dreamed about him. It was as if he had vanished from my subconscious just as he had vanished from my life.

In the dream we were back at the circus,

watching Nicholas de Frey doing his incredible trick. We were at the part where the two men circled the tank, holding the black curtain attached to long poles. I was gripped, and slowly eating my popcorn. I turned to my left, but the seat was empty. Dad was gone.

Back in the ring, the two men dropped the curtain and the audience gasped, then began to laugh.

The tank was empty of water, but someone was inside. It was Dad! He was sitting on the floor of the tank and texting on his phone.

The laughter from the audience got louder and louder when he looked up at me and waved. Faces in the crowd turned to see who he was waving at. Their laughter became louder and more maniacal. They whispered to each other, pointing at me. The girl who had been rejected by her own father.

I gasped myself awake and felt wet tears on my cheeks. I took a few long, deep breaths and calmed myself down.

Today I'd accomplished an important mission. I'd succeeded in getting Hal to a safe place. Now, I had another to crack.

I had to get hold of that letter.

CHAPTER 27

The next day at school, Matthew found me at lunchtime. I was sitting outside behind the science classrooms where it was always nice and quiet.

"Melody! Come quick! It's Jake!" he said. His face was bright red because he'd been running.

I grabbed my bag and followed him in the direction of the sports hall. The doors were wide open and there was a crowd of people, looking in.

"Mr Jenkins has really lost it this time," said Tom.

"Shouldn't we get a teacher?" said Samira.

I pushed my way to the front. Mr Jenkins had Jake backed up into a corner in the hall. He was shouting into his face.

"You don't have any RESPECT, you don't think of anyone but YOURSELF, you are a WEAK and PATHETIC person. DO YOU UNDERSTAND "WHAT I'M SAYING!" he roared. Jake was cowering against the wall.

"What happened to make him so angry?" I said.

Daniel was next to me. "Jake was supposed to be mopping the floor of the boys' changing rooms. Mr Jenkins caught him sitting down," she said.

"This is too much," I said. I turned to the crowd around me. "How can you all just watch and do nothing?"

I turned and ran to the office. Mrs Winchester was on reception and she was the worst of the admin assistants. She was eating a strawberry yoghurt, slowly scraping a teaspoon around the edges.

"Mrs Winchester! Someone needs to go to the sports hall!" I said. "Mr Jenkins is losing it with Jake!"

Mrs Winchester concentrated on her spoon. "What do you mean by 'losing it'," she said, without looking up.

"He's really angry! Can you send a teacher over immediately?" I said.

Mrs Winchester scraped at the yoghurt pot. "Everyone's at lunch and I can't leave reception. Go and find the teacher on playground duty," she said, sucking at the silver spoon.

I headed back out to the playground. I spotted Miss McClare and I ran over.

"Mr Jenkins is getting really angry with Jake," I gasped. "They're over by the sports hall and he's lost it!"

The teachers on lunchtime duty had walkie-talkies and Miss McClare quickly clicked the button on hers.

"Mr Hill? Can you pop over to the sports hall? Something is going on with Rory," she said. Mr Hill was Jake's form tutor. Maybe now someone would see what was going on?

I ran back to the sports hall, but when I got there the crowd was dispersing. Mr Hill had got there already and was standing talking to Mr Jenkins. They were both smiling. Whatever Mr Jenkins had told him had happened, Mr Hill was clearly happy with his explanation. Jake was nowhere to be seen. The bell went for next lesson. Mr Jenkins had got away with it yet again.

*

Matthew and I finally caught up with Jake as we walked home from school.

"You *have* to tell someone, Jake," I said. "He can't shout at you like that!"

"Melody is right," said Matthew. "Enough is enough. Talk to Mr Hill. Tell him what really happened."

Jake shook his head. "I'm not telling anyone," he said.

"But we'll back you up," I said. "I bet others will too!"

"There's no need. I'm sorting it," he said.

Matthew and I looked at each other.

Jake's nostrils flared. "That was the last time Rory Jenkins treats me like that," he said. "He's going to regret everything he's ever done." He climbed on to his bike and rode off.

"I don't like the sound of that, do you?" said Matthew. I agreed. I didn't want Jake to end up in even more trouble.

When we got to Chestnut Close, Jake was standing talking to Old Nina outside number one. For a moment I was worried she was asking him about Hal, but he just shook his head at her and walked to his front door.

I approached her nervously. "Is everything all right, Nina?" I said. Old Nina's hands were clenched in front of her.

"Oh, hello, Melody," she said. "I've lost my brooch. The one that Walter gave to me on my sixtieth birthday. Have you seen it?"

I knew which one she meant. It was blue and shaped like a daisy. She'd had it pinned to her jumper when we'd seen her the night we moved Hal into number one.

"No. Sorry, Nina," I said.

"Have you been out today at all?" said Matthew.

"I went to the shops earlier and I've looked all along the pavement but I can't find it anywhere," she said. "I think it's gone." Her pale grey eyes looked shiny with tears. It was horrible seeing her looking so upset.

"How about calling the shops that you went into to see if anyone has handed it in?" I said. She brightened a little.

"That's a good idea. I'll do that right now," she said. She hurried back home. When she was out of hearing range, Matthew turned to me. His eyes were wide.

"Come back to mine for a minute," he said. He

let us in with his key and threw his school bag on to the stairs, then closed the door behind us.

"Melody. Do you remember what happened last night when we moved Hal? And what he said to Old Nina?"

I thought about it.

"Um, he said something about her house looking like a vampire lived there," I said.

"And did you notice where he was standing? He moved and stood right beside Old Nina when he was talking."

I remembered that. I hadn't thought anything of it.

"What are you saying, Matthew?" I said.

"I'm saying that when he started talking about vampires and her house, it was just a misdirection. Like the magic trick he showed us with the pebble! He was taking the attention away from himself while he stole Old Nina's brooch!" said Matthew.

I felt a knot in my chest and my throat tightened.

"I don't think Hal is working for MI8 after all," he said. "I think he's a thief!"

A thief! The words rang in my head like a fire alarm.

"But he can't be!" I said.

Matthew looked sad for me, which made me feel even more upset.

"I'm sorry, Melody," he said. "I think you need to consider that Hal isn't all that he says he is."

My legs felt like they were going to give way. I sat myself on the bottom of Matthew's stairs. This was my worst nightmare. Hal could be a fraud. Just like my dad.

"Melody? Are you OK?" said Matthew. He crouched down beside me. "What's wrong?"

"I can't be lied to again, Matthew. I just can't," I said.

"What do you mean?" said Matthew. "Who lied to you, Melody?"

I sniffed and gulped at the same time. "Dad," I said. "He . . . he lied to us. Really badly."

I didn't want to cry, but I felt a tear roll down my cheek. I quickly wiped it away.

"What happened?" he asked.

I closed my eyes, counted to three. When I was certain I wouldn't start sobbing, I opened them again.

"Melody?" said Matthew. "Talking about it might help, you know."

He was right. I couldn't feel any worse, that

was for sure.

"My dad is the biggest liar I've ever known," I said. Matthew waited for me to continue. I took a few deep breaths and began.

"Dad took me to the circus once. We saw a brilliant magician called Nicholas de Frey. He was an underwater escapologist and he did an incredible routine where he was cuffed and chained up in a tank of water. When the curtain dropped the tank was empty. He had completely disappeared! It was brilliant! The best thing I've ever seen."

Matthew smiled and stayed silent.

"After the trick finished, Dad said we had to leave, even though the show wasn't over. We headed to the car and Dad walked a few paces in front of me, talking on his mobile. I couldn't make out what he was saying but I was pretty sure that he didn't want me to hear. Every time I tried to catch him up he turned his head to one side."

I could feel my throat tighten again.

"When we got home, everything seemed normal. I went to bed happy and trying to work out how Nicholas de Frey had disappeared from the water tank. I mean, how could someone just vanish like that?" I smiled. "It was the next day when everything changed."

"How did it change?" said Matthew, his eyes wide.

I took another deep breath.

"I went downstairs the next morning and Mum was sitting in the kitchen, crying. She had a letter in her hand. She was shaking her head and saying, 'I never knew. All these years and I never knew.'

"I remembered it so clearly. There had been something scrunched-up on the floor. I picked it up. It was a photograph. I smoothed out the creases and looked at the picture. It was a family of three, sitting at a table. In the middle was a woman with a baby on her lap. The baby had a dark mop of hair and was leaning forwards towards a large cake that was on the table. The cake had a single burning candle. I read the piped icing:

Happy 1st Birthday Maisie!

"The woman had dark, bobbed hair, brown eyes and a big, wide smile. It looked like a very happy moment, captured forever with the snap of a camera."

I took a deep, shuddering breath. "But then I

looked at the man who was standing behind them. I felt like I was going to be sick, right there and then. The man was my dad. He was wearing the same smile that I'd seen so many times; the one he wore when he came home from a business trip and was really happy to see us. He had his arm around the woman. And he was smiling down at the baby."

I stopped talking for a moment. My legs were trembling and I clutched my knees with my hands.

"The letter in Mum's hand was from the woman in the photograph. She said that Dad had been living a double life. He wasn't away on business trips at all, he was living with this other woman and they had a baby together: Maisie. The woman found out about us by accident. At first, she was really angry. But then she told him he had to decide, once and for all, who he wanted to be with."

Matthew blinked.

"I didn't realize, but the circus was just a 'goodbye' trip for me. The woman posted the letter to Mum while we were out, just to make sure she knew exactly what was going on and that Dad was going to go through with it. Mum texted Dad and told him she knew everything." I closed my eyes and swallowed. "He chose her, Matthew. He chose the other woman," I said. "And he chose Maisie. He didn't want me."

I opened my eyes again and took a breath.

"The next day, Dad vanished from our lives. Just like Nicholas de Frey vanished from that tank," I said. The tears began again and this time I let them come. Matthew stayed silent as I cried. "I'll never forgive him," I said. "And that's why I don't like liars."

"I'm so sorry, Melody," said Matthew. "That must have been awful."

I nodded. It hurt so much to remember all of this, but it also felt good to cry and let it all out.

"And there's more," I said. "Dad has written a letter to Mr Charles. I saw it when I was getting the key to number one."

"What did it say?" he said.

"I only read the beginning before Mum came in," I said. "I told her it was post for Mr Charles so she took it back. He can't have realized it was post he already had, thankfully. I can't ask to see it or he'll know I've been snooping around."

"Why didn't you tell me this was going on?" asked Matthew.

"I didn't think you'd care," I said.

Matthew looked mortified. I thought he was

going to object or say I had been imagining it, but he just took a deep breath. "You're right. I haven't always been the best friend to you, have I? I'm sorry, Melody."

I took a tissue out of my pocket and blew my nose.

"Melody?" he said. "That letter from your dad in Mr Charles's house. I'll get it for you."

"Really?" I said. "You'd do that?"

Matthew nodded. "And I know just the person who might be able to help."

I couldn't think who he meant.

"Who?" I said.

"Casey," he said, with a grin. "But first, we need to talk to Hal about Old Nina's brooch. Come on. Let's go and see him."

CHAPTER 28

I really hoped Hal wasn't involved in the disappearance of Old Nina's brooch. If he was, then everything was over. We'd call the police and all of Hal's lies would be out in the open. But I didn't know that they *were* lies. I still hoped he was telling the truth.

When we walked out of Matthew's house, Hannah was putting Max into his car seat in the back of her car. She waved and we both waved back. We pretended to stop and chat on Matthew's door step then, as soon as she'd driven away we hurried across the road and up the path of number one. I looked around, then quickly unlocked the door and we went inside.

Hal was in the kitchen, holding an open packet of biscuits.

"Oh good! It's you!" he said with a smile. "Have you found another message, Melody?"

With so much going on I'd completely forgotten about checking the grave. "I haven't looked yet," I said. "We need to talk to you about something first. Something important."

Matthew folded his arms.

"Stealing biscuits as well now, are you?" said Matthew.

Hal's face dropped and he put the biscuit down. "They were in the cupboard," he said. "They're out of date, I thought it would be OK."

Matthew ignored him. "Did you take Old Nina's brooch?" he said.

"What?" said Hal. "I don't know what you're talking about."

"Old Nina lost a valuable piece of jewellery yesterday. A brooch. And *you* were right there when she was wearing it," I said. "Hal, have you been lying to me about being a spy?"

Hal looked startled. "Would I make this up, Melody Bird? This is my job!"

A tight, panicky feeling was in my chest. The one I had felt in the weeks after Dad had left.

"You made that pebble disappear when you were showing off your magic skills yesterday," said Matthew. "Did you make that brooch disappear too? Old Nina's dead husband gave her that brooch!"

"I don't understand," said Hal. "What's going on? Melody?"

He looked so upset I nearly told Matthew that we'd made a mistake. But I held fast. Something was clearly wrong here. "We just have a lot of unanswered questions. That's all," I said.

Suddenly the doorbell rang and someone thumped on the glass. We all froze.

"It's him!" cried Hal. "It's the criminals! Martin Stone has found me!"

Very slowly, I turned around. There was the outline of someone on the step. And they were holding something in their arms.

"That's no criminal," I said. I opened the door. Jake Bishop was standing in front of me. In his arms was a white, fluffy bundle. It was Wilson, the puppy.

"Jake! What on earth are you doing?" I said.

"Let me in!" he said. "Quick!" He rushed down the hallway and I glanced around the close and shut the door. I went to the kitchen. Wilson was wriggling in Jake's arms, trying to lick his face.

"Get off ... Get OFF!" said Jake.

"Jake!" said Matthew. "Why have you got Wilson?"

Jake put the little dog down on to the floor. Wilson scampered excitedly between us. He sniffed at our ankles and rushed from person to person. He got to Hal and jumped up at his legs. Hal knelt down and ruffled his fur before he scampered off to see me, then Matthew, then Jake. He was like a fluffy ball in a pinball machine.

"Jake?" I said. "Please tell me you haven't done what I think you've done."

Jake was breathing fast. He looked a bit like he was in shock.

"It all happened so fast," he said. "Hannah went out and Wilson was in the back garden yapping. She must have forgotten to lock him inside. I went out into our garden, reached over the fence and just ... took him."

"You kidnapped Wilson?" I said. The puppy was so excited his little face was practically beaming at us.

"Actually, I think it's called dognapped, not kidnapped," said Hal.

"Mr Jenkins is going to kill you!" said Matthew.

Wilson's little tail was wagging so much he couldn't walk in a straight line. He scampered off to the lounge and Jake went after him.

Matthew looked at me and raised his eyebrows, and then we followed. Wilson was lying on the sofa on his back, his tummy bare, ready to be tickled.

"Do you know, I think this is the longest he's gone without barking," said Jake. He sat beside the little dog and began to rub his tummy. Considering how much he supposedly hated Wilson, he seemed rather taken with him.

"Go home and put Wilson back over the fence right now and then no one will ever know what you did," said Matthew. "Hannah and Mr Jenkins are both out."

"But he's made my life so miserable. He *deserves* this. He deserves for his precious puppy to 'disappear'," said Jake.

"You haven't thought this through!" I said. "He'll start barking before long and give you away! And what about Hal? We can't risk drawing attention to this house. You've *got* to put him back!"

Jake looked at me and then at Hal. "You don't still believe the rubbish he's been telling you?" he said. "He's a liar, Melody. Why can't you see it? Why can't you both see it?" He glared at us. "You do know that Old Nina's brooch has gone missing, don't you? Do you think that's a coincidence: it disappears on the day that *he* comes here? Really?"

"We were trying to get to the bottom of that before you turned up," I said. "Stealing Wilson is just going to make everything worse for you, Jake. Just take him back and no one will ever know."

Jake continued to stroke Wilson, scowling. "OK," he said. "But I'm not doing it for *him*, OK? He's a lying thief."

Hal didn't say anything. Jake stood up and lifted Wilson into his arms. Wilson immediately gave him a big slobbery lick across one cheek.

"Urgh, come on, you stupid mutt. Fun time is over," he said.

But Matthew shook his head. He was standing by the lounge window looking out.

"Too late," he said. "Look."

Behind him and through the net curtains

we could see Mr Jenkins walking up his path, unlocking his front door and going inside.

For now, Wilson would just have to stay.

CHAPTER 29

There was no way Jack could put the puppy back now that Mr Jenkins was home. And it would only be a matter of time before he realized his dog was missing. Jake sat back down and Wilson settled in his lap.

"Now what do we do?" said Matthew.

Hal went out to the kitchen and came back holding the packet of biscuits he had found earlier. "Does anyone want a biscuit?" he said. He held them out to me and Matthew. We both shook our heads. He walked over to Jake on the sofa.

"Do you want one, Jake? They look really nice," he said.

"I don't think this is the time for tea and biscuits, do you?" said Jake. Wilson got a sniff of the biscuits, got down off Jake's lap and jumped up Hal's legs. Hal held one out to him and Wilson practically swallowed it whole.

"Don't give him those!" said Jake. "Sugar isn't good for dogs. Don't you know anything?"

"Oh, sorry," said Hal. He took a biscuit out for himself. A few crumbs dropped on to the carpet and Wilson quickly licked them up.

"Wilson! Here boy!" said Jake. "Leave the biscuits!"

The little puppy looked up at him then scampered over, diving back on to his lap.

"I've a few questions for you, *Hal*," said Jake. "How can you be spy when you don't look old enough to drive? And if you're a spy, where are your team? Your contacts? Why haven't you called someone? Why would you need a bunch of kids to help you?" Wilson span around on Jake's lap and then put his little paws up on to his shoulders, giving his face another big lick.

"Urgh. Wilson!" he said. "Not again!"

"I've already explained everything to Melody," said Hal.

"Fine. So, explain it to me," said Jake.

Hal took an impatient breath.

"It's hard, because I have to be careful about how much I tell you. MI8 are involved in various missions around the UK. They are based not far from here and . . . are you all right?"

Jake looked flushed. He wiped at his forehead with his sleeve.

"Yes," he snapped. "I'm fine."

"OK. So they're an anti-crime organisation who aren't known because they don't want to be. The Warley Tower branch, where I am based, are attempting to arrest Martin Stone, the criminal I told you about. He's a high-profile thief who has evaded capture for years but in the last few weeks... Are you *sure* you're all right? You really don't look well at all," said Hal, taking a step towards Jake.

Jake's face was bright red now and his eyes were beginning to water. He lifted Wilson off his lap and slowly stood up.

"Jake? What's happening?" I said. I noticed his lips were beginning to swell.

"He's having an allergic reaction!" I shouted.

Matthew grabbed the packet from Hal's hand and searched for the ingredients.

"They've got nuts in, you *idiot*!" he said.

"But he didn't have one," said Hal.

Jake had his hand to his throat, trying to swallow. He looked utterly terrified.

"Where's your EpiPen, Jake?" I said. Jake always carried it with him in a little sports bag, but there was no sign of it.

"We've got to get him home!" said Matthew. "His mum will have an EpiPen there. We need to carry him." Jake put his arms over our shoulders and we lifted his legs and carried him to the hallway. I managed to open the door and we got him down the step and outside.

We'd made it to the pavement with Wilson barking and running around us in circles. The door of number one closed behind us just as the door of number seven opened.

"WHAT THE HELL ARE YOU DOING WITH MY DOG!" yelled Mr Jenkins across the close at us.

"It's all right, Jake. We've got you!" said Matthew. We got to Jake's house and sat him at the end of his driveway. Mr Jenkins stormed across the road and scooped Wilson up.

"Mr Jenkins! Call an ambulance! He's having an allergic reaction!" said Matthew.

Mr Jenkins ignored him and stuck his face inches from Jake's.

"Are you behind this, Bishop? What is *wrong* with you?" he said.

"Mr Jenkins!" I cried. "You've got to call for help!"

"Don't give me that rubbish," sneered Mr Jenkins at me. "Look at him! He's clearly faking it. Isn't the whole 'allergy routine' a bit tired by now?"

Jake began to make weird, gasping sounds and I saw Mr Jenkins falter for a split second. But he didn't do anything. Jake was suffering, right in front of his eyes, but he did nothing. That was when I saw Sheila, Matthew's mum, appear behind him.

"Mum!" called Matthew. "Jake needs his EpiPen! Get Sue and call an ambulance!"

Sheila sprinted off, pulling her mobile out of her back pocket. As she ran she shouted out:

"I heard you, Rory Jenkins! I heard EVERYTHING!" she yelled. "Hannah will be so ashamed of you. DO YOU HEAR ME? ASHAMED!"

I watched as Mr Jenkins's Adam's apple rose and fell in his taut throat. Then he backed away from us, all the way to his front door.

Sheila pounded on the door of number five and

Sue appeared with a worried look on her face. She turned and ran to the kitchen, quickly reappearing with a plastic ziplocked wallet in her hand. Jake was making an awful, wheezing noise and his eyes were streaming.

"Mum?" he croaked.

"It's OK, I've got it. Don't worry, darling," said Sue. She took a cylindrical object out of the wallet and popped off the blue lid. It looked exactly like a chunky ink pen. Sheila was talking to the emergency services on her mobile.

Jake leaned back against their front wall and Sue got on to her knees. She gripped the pen and pressed the end against Jake's trousers on his thigh, jabbing it hard. It made a loud click. She held it there for a few seconds as we all watched.

Sue stroked Jake's hair.

"The EpiPen is working now, darling," she said. "You're going to be fine. The ambulance is coming."

"Sue? Is everything OK?" Mum came running out of our house and joined us.

Jake looked dreadful. His eyes were puffy and his cheeks were bright red. His lips had swollen so much that his face didn't look like his any more.

But he was breathing more easily.

Matthew stood beside me, his hands trembling.

"You were brilliant, Matthew," I said, quietly. "I'm so proud of you." We were both shaking.

"He knew, Melody," Matthew said. "Hal knew that Jake was allergic."

I stared at him. He was right. Hal *had* known about Jake's allergies. He'd called them "severe" when we'd all been in the plague house.

"And? What are you saying?" I whispered. I could hear the noise of sirens in the distance. The ambulance was coming. Old Nina was watching everything from her front window. Mr Charles came out with Teddy in his arms and Casey by his side. He went and stood with Sheila.

"I think Hal might be more than a thief," Matthew went on. "I think he might have manipulated this whole thing. Jake was the one who threatened to go to the police, who was asking all the awkward questions. Then, do you remember how keen he was to offer those biscuits round?"

I felt sick. "But Jake didn't take one," I said. "Hal didn't cause this."

"No, he didn't. But Wilson ate one, didn't he? And then he licked Jake's face," said Matthew. "I think Hal did his best to hurt Jake."

I followed Matthew's gaze. As we watched, the silhouette of Hal slowly moved away from the window. What he was suggesting was awful. Surely it wasn't true?

"Melody," said Matthew. "I think Hal Vincent might be dangerous."

CHAPTER 30

When the ambulance arrived, Mum stood to one side with Sheila and Mr Charles. They were talking in hushed voices, looking at Mr Jenkins's house, who still hadn't reappeared.

The ambulance took Sue and Jake to hospital and all of the neighbours headed back to their houses. Mum put her arm around me as we walked to our door.

"You and Matthew were very brave," she said, giving me a little squeeze. "Poor Jake. That must have been very frightening."

I felt like I wanted to cry. Everything had

happened so quickly. Mum closed our front door and Frankie came trotting down the hallway to say hello. I picked him up and gave him a cuddle.

"Sheila said that Rory Jenkins didn't believe that Jake was sick," said Mum. "She said he was saying all sorts of nasty things to him?"

I nodded.

"Yes. He shouted at him. He's really not nice to Jake, Mum," I said. "It's been going on for a while now. He picks on him at school."

Mum frowned. "OK," she said. "Sheila is going to talk to Sue when she can and also speak to your school about him. I'll have to have a word with Hannah, I think."

That *was* good news. Mr Jenkins was going to be exposed as a bully at last.

Around ten p.m. I got a text from Matthew saying that Jake was still at the hospital, but Sue had texted his mum to say he was improving.

I texted back saying that I was pleased he was OK. There was a bit of a pause and then Matthew replied.

> We need to tell the police about Hal. Whatever happened with Old Nina's brooch and with

> Jake, there are too many questions. This has gone far enough.

I stared at my phone.
I kept thinking back to the moment when Hal had offered the biscuits around. Had he really been trying to hurt Jake? I typed my reply.

> Anything could have happened to Old Nina's brooch. And I'm pretty sure what happened to Jake was an accident, Matty.

There was a pause, and then Matthew's answer popped on to my screen.

> How sure? 100%?

He was right. I couldn't be a hundred per cent certain. But I still didn't think that the boy in the plague house, who had shown me magic tricks and asked for my help in a criminal investigation, had tried to physically harm Jake. And part of me, a very big part, still wanted to believe that he was a spy. That he hadn't lied to me.

There was one way that I could find out the

truth. I could try and solve the Martin Stone case and find the missing necklace. Then we would know for sure.

> We can go to the police. I need to do one more thing to try and solve this case first though. Just a bit more time. Please?

I stared at my phone for another twenty minutes, but Matthew didn't reply.

There was probably a riddle waiting to be found right this very second. I *had* to check as soon as possible. I knew that Mum wouldn't let me go to the graveyard this late. I had to make another night-time visit there. But this time, I would go on my own.

After I heard Mum go to bed I waited for another twenty minutes, then got up. I pulled on my dressing gown and tiptoed downstairs. This time, Frankie heard me. His claws clicked across the kitchen floor as he got up to see what was going on. When he saw me, his tail began to wag, his eyes blinking and winking from being woken up.

"Go back to sleep, Frankie," I said, stroking his long ears. "It's not time for a walk. I'll be back soon."

He sat down and watched as I quickly put on my trainers and picked up my key from the side table. I opened the door and stepped out into the night.

The graveyard was much darker than it had been when Matthew and I had gone to get Hal. The sky was cloudy and there was no bright moon shining down to light the way. I looked around at the dark-grey, cold headstones and wished I had the torch I lent to Hal. Shadows swayed this way and that and, for a second, I imagined that they were the shadows of the dead, come out at night to dance amongst the graves then returning back to their tombs before daylight. I shivered.

"Don't start thinking like that, Melody," I said to myself. "Come on, you've got a job to do."

The white headstones in the newer part of the cemetery seemed to give off a welcome glow of light. I sped up, hurrying to the grave where Martin Stone had been leaving the notes and supposedly watering his dead wife's roses. Every now and then I checked behind me. It felt like I was being watched, but each time I looked there was nobody there.

I got to the gravestone and stopped. This was the exact spot where Martin Stone had been standing when I had first seen him, standing under a red umbrella. I glanced at the inscription on the headstone.

> *In loving memory of Margaret Young.*
> *Beloved wife, mother and grandmother.*

That was weird. She didn't have "Stone" as her surname. Maybe she hadn't taken his name? I checked around the grave and there it was. Tucked between the headstone and the soil, was a note. I grabbed it, brushed the dirt off, and began to read.

> The man who made it did not want it; the man who bought it did not use it; the man who used it did not know it.

It didn't make any sense. I read it three more times, made certain I'd memorized it exactly, then put it back where I found it.

CHAPTER 31

The next morning was Friday. Mum had made a pile of toast and laid out the table with tea, butter, jam, honey and marmalade. I didn't say anything as I sat down, helping myself to a piece of toast.

"Morning, love," said Mum. "Are you OK?"

"Morning," I said. "Yes. I'm fine."

She sat down opposite me and I did a big yawn. "Sue texted and said that they got home from the hospital in the early hours of this morning," she said. "Jake is worn out but much better now. She also said that they are going to school first thing to talk about Mr Jenkins."

At last. He was going to get his comeuppance.

"Do you know what caused Jake's reaction?" Mum said. I looked up. She stared at me and put her mug of tea down.

"It must have been something he'd eaten I guess," I said. I scraped butter across a piece of toast then cut it into triangles.

Mum picked her mug up again and took a sip. She kept looking at me. I ate half a slice of toast, then stood up and brushed the crumbs from my school skirt.

"Before you go, Melody, there's something I need to tell you," said Mum. "We've had an offer on the house. It's a good one and I've decided to accept."

My stomach tightened. I didn't reply.

"I know you don't want to move," said Mum. "But like I said before, the reality is that we can't afford to stay here any longer."

"How could you do this to me, Mum?" I said. "Dad lied to us and hurt us both so much, and now you've lied too!"

Mum shook her head. "I haven't lied, Melody."

"Keeping secrets from me is the same as lying. Especially with something this big!" I said.

Mum looked down at her tea. "I'm sorry, Melody. I am only trying to do what is best for us," she said. She really did look upset.

"If you want to do what's best for us, then why aren't you asking Dad for help? He hasn't paid for anything since he left, has he?" I said.

Mum shook her head. "I don't want anything from him," she said. "He made his choice. He isn't a part of this family any more."

I thought about the letter in Mr Charles's house. Matthew had said he would get it for me. If he did, I thought, then I could contact Dad myself.

"I've got to go or I'm going to be late," I said. And I walked out of the kitchen without looking at her.

When I got to school, there was a crowd of pupils hanging around the staff car park. They were filming something on their phones.

"And you'd take his word OVER MINE? THIS IS ABSURD!" It was Mr Jenkins. And he was shouting at our headmistress, Mrs Blakemore. I spotted Matthew in the crowd, standing slightly apart, and went over to join him.

"What's going on?"

"Sue has made an official complaint against Mr Jenkins. My mum has also made a statement about what she heard him say," he said. "Apparently, Mrs Blakemore was talking to him in her office and he just lost it. He was asked to leave the premises while they investigate what happened but he only got as far as the car park."

Mrs Blakemore was standing with her arms out, like she was trying to coax an angry bear to calm down.

"Mr Jenkins," she was saying. "I don't think that this is the time or place to discuss this, do you? Be sensible about this, please."

"Sensible? You've taken a kid's word over mine!"

Someone pointed across the car park to the main reception.

"Look! There's Jake!"

Jake came out of the main doors with his mum. He wasn't in school uniform so I guessed he was taking the day off considering how unwell he'd been yesterday. Mr Jenkins pointed straight at him.

"Ah, and here he is! The little actor himself. Going to put on another drama, are you, Bishop? Going to make up more lies?"

"MR JENKINS! This is really not appropriate behaviour for a member of our teaching staff," shouted Mrs Blakemore.

Mr Jenkins's face was red with rage. "Well, in that case, I QUIT!" he said.

There was a sharp intake of breath from the crowd. Had that really happened? Had Mr Jenkins actually resigned, right there and then in the car park? We all looked around at each other in disbelief, and then someone began to clap. At first, it was very quiet; but then someone else joined in, and then another, and another. It didn't take long until every single student standing there was applauding. A few people even began to cheer. I looked over at Jake and Sue who were standing on the path, watching.

Mr Jenkins stood motionless. His jaw dangled down as he stared as everyone. Then he shook his head and stormed off out of the car park. The show was over.

The bell went and Mrs Blakemore went to talk to Sue. Jake came over to us.

"Hi, Jake. How are you feeling?" I said. His skin was pale with red blotches and his eyes were still swollen, but he looked much better than yesterday.

"I'm OK," he said.

"It's good news about Mr Jenkins, isn't it?" I said.

"Yep, he won't be teaching here again, that's for sure. Or probably anywhere else for that matter," said Matthew.

But rather than looking happy, Jake just looked tired.

"Have you got the day off?" I said.

Jake nodded.

"Yeah. We're going back to the doctor. Mum's worried I've got another allergy that we don't know about," he said. "I told her I hadn't eaten anything so we don't know what caused it."

I looked at Matthew and he looked at me.

"Jake. There were nuts in the biscuit that Hal offered to you," said Matthew. Jake frowned.

"But I didn't have one?" he said.

"No, but Wilson licked your face after *he'd* eaten one. Do you remember?" Matthew said. "That must have caused the reaction."

Jake thought about it, and then his eyes widened. "Hang on. He *knew* I had allergies but he offered me a biscuit anyway!" he said.

"It wasn't Hal's fault," I said. "There's no reason he'd want to harm you!"

Jake glared at me. "Are you sure about that?" he said.

"Of course I'm sure!" I said. Jake didn't look convinced. "Well, I don't think he'd do something like this on purpose," I said. "We owe it to him to hear his side first. Don't we?"

"I don't owe him anything," said Jake. He looked over at his mum who was now heading towards us. "I'm going to go and have it out with him tomorrow before the Big Graveyard Clear-up," he said. "If I don't like what I hear, then Hal is *finished*."

CHAPTER 32

The next morning was Saturday. Mum was up early. When I went into the kitchen she was wearing an old T-shirt and some scruffy yoga pants, and she had a scarf tied around her hair. On the table were two canvas bags filled with a selection of tools and gardening gloves. Beside those was a large, plastic tub full of chocolate brownies from the café.

"Morning, darling. I thought we could do with a good, wholesome breakfast to keep us going at the Big Graveyard Clear-up," said Mum, slicing some banana into two cereal bowls filled with muesli. "How did you sleep?"

"All right," I lied. I felt like I hadn't slept at all. I was so worried about what Jake would do when he spoke to Hal. I wanted to be there so I could smooth things over.

I picked up the cereal bowl and sat at the table.

"Mum? Do I have to help today?"

Mum frowned. "Why? What's the matter, Melody?" she said.

"I just don't feel like it," I said. I scraped at the muesli with my spoon.

Mum sat down opposite me. "But we've told Mr Charles we'll both be there," she said. "We don't want to let him down." My stomach knotted.

"But you can go on your own," I said, not looking at her.

Mum was quiet for a bit. "What's the matter, Melody?" she said. "Is this about the move? I know it's really hard. You can talk to me, you know."

It was Hal, Dad's letter, having to move house, and now Jake. It was *everything*. I could feel Mum's eyes on me.

"It's nice to do something for the neighbourhood, don't you think?" she said.

"What neighbourhood?" I shouted. "You want

to move, remember? You don't want to *be* a part of this neighbourhood any more!"

Mum sighed and stood up. "I want you to help today, Melody. Just like we said we would," she said. "Mr Charles is expecting both of us to be there."

"OK," I said with a huff. "I'll come."

"Good. I'll see you there," she said. "Don't be too long. I'll take Frankie with me now." She went to the hallway and Frankie followed when he heard his lead jingle. The door banged shut behind them. I left my breakfast and ran upstairs to get dressed.

I checked through the window of our door, making sure the coast was clear, then I walked quickly out of our house and up the pathway to number one.

As soon as I got inside, I went through to the kitchen.

"Hal? Are you here? Hal!" I called. I went to the lounge, where Hal was on the sofa covered in the blankets.

"Melody?" he croaked. He sat up and rubbed his eyes. "How's Jake?" he said.

"He's fine now," I said. "There were nuts in

the biscuit that you gave to Wilson. And then Wilson licked Jake's face and set off an allergic reaction."

"Oh no, that's awful," said Hal, frowning. "Is he OK?"

I studied him as he spoke. "Yes. But it was very serious for a moment," I said. "Hal? Did you know Jake had a nut allergy?"

His forehead wrinkled. "No. You said he had allergies but not what they were. I should have checked the ingredients, I guess. I'm sorry, Melody Bird."

He did seem genuinely upset.

"Well, he's OK now, luckily," I said. "But Matthew and Jake think you tried to give him a biscuit on purpose. I think they're going to tell someone about you. Unless you show them some proof you are who you say you are."

Hal sat up even more. He was wide awake now. "But I've done that," he said, quietly. He pulled up his knees and wrapped his arms around them. "I told Matthew all about MI8's interest in hiring him. You believe me, don't you?"

I looked at the sad boy sitting on the sofa, wrapped in his blankets. My throat felt dry when I swallowed.

"I . . . I don't know any more," I said.

The doorbell went and Hal jumped. "W-who's that?" he said. He looked frozen with fear.

"It's Jake and Matthew," I said. "You need to convince them, Hal. Or it's all over."

I ran to let them in. Jake stormed past me.

"Where is he?" he shouted. He went into the lounge and Matthew and I quickly followed.

"Let's sort this out once and for all, shall we?" said Jake. "It's time to find out who you really are." He grabbed Hal's rucksack.

"No!" said Hal. He kicked the blankets off and jumped up. "Give it back!"

He grabbed one of the straps and pulled it, but Jake quickly snatched it away and undid the zip.

He tipped the contents of the rucksack out on to the carpet and everything fell out in a heap. In the pile I spotted the red, woolly cardigan that Hal had been wearing when I met him, a comb, the torch, Matthew's binoculars and a white envelope.

I picked it up. It was something from the town council. On the front was a typed name and address.

H Vincent
408 Warley Tower
SX13 2LP

Warley Tower! This must be post addressed to MI8's headquarters! He *was* telling the truth! MI8 *did* exist!

"Look! Warley Tower!" I said. "See? He's telling the truth!" But Hal snatched the envelope from me.

"That's mine!" he said, stuffing it into his jeans pocket.

Jake dived on to his knees and began to go through everything.

"These are yours for a start," Jake said, holding the binoculars out to Matthew.

"But Melody got those for me," said Hal. "I didn't steal them!"

"He's right, Jake. I borrowed them," I said. Jake ignored me. Hal made a feeble attempt to grapple some of his things back but Jake easily pushed him on to the sofa.

"I don't understand," said Hal. He wrapped his arms tightly around himself. "I'm Special Agent Hal Vincent. I'm not a criminal!"

He looked so sad.

"Jake, that's enough," I said. "You're upsetting him."

Jake threw the items to one side. "Ah, now this is more like it. Who did you steal this from, eh?" Jake held up the black digital watch. Hal's eyes widened and he began to breathe heavily through his nose.

"GIVE IT BACK," he said.

Jake waved it at him. "Stole it from some poor unsuspecting victim, did you? You make me sick!" he said.

Neither of them moved for a moment, and then Hal lurched towards the watch in Jake's outstretched hand. Jake quickly switched it to the other hand and put it behind his back.

"Come on, Jake," said Matthew. "That's enough now, eh?"

But Jake wasn't listening. He held the watch behind his back, moving it into his other hand every time Hal tried to grab it.

"Jake, cut it out!" I said. Hal just looked more and more desperate, trying to grab at the watch.

"It's not what you think it is!" I shouted. "It belongs to MI8. It's a communication device."

Jake stopped and stared at the plastic watch in his palm. "You're joking," he said. He looked at it closely. "It's just a cheap piece of rubbish."

"It's not RUBBISH. My mum gave that to me!" shouted Hal. He took another leap towards Jake's hand, but the watch flew into the air and smashed against the wall.

"No!" cried Hal. He fell to his knees and stared at the shattered pieces on the floor. Then he began to frantically pick up every tiny shard of glass and plastic. Some were so small you could barely see them. When every piece had been collected he cupped them in his hands and began to cry.

My mouth hung open as I watched him.

"Hal? Are you OK?" I said.

I looked at Jake and Matthew. They both looked just as baffled.

"Hal? What did you mean, your mum gave you that watch?" I said.

Hal kept his head down, sobbing quietly.

I looked at Matthew. "I think you two should go now," I said.

Jake looked shaken by Hal's reaction but he wasn't going to leave it.

"He's lying," he said quietly. "About everything."

"Come on, Jake," said Matthew. "Melody's right.

Let's just leave it for now."

The two of them turned and went out of the lounge. I heard the front door click quietly behind them.

I slowly began to collect Hal's things and put them back into his rucksack. I folded up his red cardigan and put that on the bottom. On top of that I put his thin trousers and a pair of pants and socks. I put Matthew's binoculars to one side and carried on putting the other things away.

"There we are," I said. "That's everything put away."

I looked at the boy who was crouched on the floor, hugging his knees as he cried.

"Hal, are you OK? You're frightening me," I said.

Very slowly he lifted his head. His eyes were red around the rims and his cheeks were blotchy. He looked at me, but his face had a puzzled expression. It was as if he'd just been woken up from a very long sleep.

"I . . . I . . ." he stammered.

I knelt down beside him and put my hand on his arm.

"Please, tell me what's wrong?" I said.

He blinked at me. The tears had stopped

now. I watched as he swallowed and took a long, calming breath.

"I don't know who I am," he said.

CHAPTER 33

At first, I thought it was some kind of bizarre joke. I waited for the punchline, but he just stared at me. He was waiting for me to answer.

"What do you mean?" I said. "You're Special Agent Hal Vincent. You work with the Warley Tower branch of MI8."

Hal just stared at me, confused. He looked back down at the broken watch.

"I think you might be in some kind of shock. You've been under a terrible amount of stress lately. Just take some deep breaths, OK? Slow and steady."

My phone bleeped and I quickly took it out of my pocket. It was Mum.

Where are you, Melody? Everybody is here! x

"Listen, I've got to go. But I'll come back in a couple of hours and check on you, OK? I found the riddle, by the gravestone, and we can try and solve it. *Then* we might be able to solve the case and find the Kingfisher Necklace. That will prove to Matthew and Jake once and for all that you're who you say you are! Won't that be great?"

Hal was taking deep breaths like I said. He didn't say anything.

"I'll come back as soon as I can," I said. "Just try and relax, OK?"

He nodded. I hesitated for a moment, then got up and went to the door. I quickly ducked out and ran across the close. There was no fear that I'd be spotted this time. Everyone would be in the graveyard.

Everyone, that was, except Rory Jenkins. When I got there, there was no sign of him in the crowd of people getting ready to start work. There were a few faces I recognized from a nearby street and about fifteen of us in all.

I spotted Hannah with Max in a baby carrier on her chest. He was kicking his feet and gurgling.

Wilson was yapping and spinning around on his lead by her feet. She was in deep conversation with Matthew's mum, Sheila. Sheila kept rubbing her arm and nodding.

Mum gave me a wave and I waved back. I went and stood by Jake and Matthew.

"What on earth just happened?" said Matthew. "He went so *weird*."

"Of course he did! Jake broke his watch, did he?" I said, sharply. "That watch was a really important part of his mission."

"His mission?!" said Jake. "Come on, Melody. He's hiding something!"

I didn't reply. Time was running out. There was no way Jake or Matthew would keep quiet for much longer. Hal and I had to solve the case and fast.

Old Nina appeared beside us. It was a warm day and she had her jacket over her arm. She was wearing a red and white spotty dress and, pinned to one side, was her sparkly blue brooch.

"Hello, Nina," I said. "You found your brooch!"

I looked at Matthew and Jake and raised my eyebrows at them.

"Yes, it was such a relief! I did what you suggested,

Melody, and rang round the shops. Someone had handed it in at the newsagents. People can be so kind, don't you think?" She smiled and walked off to help Brian with the refreshments table.

I turned to Jake. "See?" I said. "I told you Hal had nothing to do with it!"

Jake just shrugged. "OK. Maybe he didn't take the brooch but he's definitely up to something."

"Hey, Melody. Did you hear about Mr Jenkins?" said Matthew. I shook my head. "He's gone. Mum spoke to Hannah and he's moved all of his stuff out. Maybe for good."

"Poor Hannah and Max," I said. "I hope they're OK."

To my surprise, Hannah waved at Jake who went over. She passed him Wilson's lead and he came back to us with the puppy bounding around at his feet.

"I said I'd look after Wilson for her today. It looks like she's got her hands full, what with the baby and everything," he said. I looked at Matthew and he grinned. Jake bent down and ruffled the fluffy hair on the top of Wilson's head. The dog's pink tongue spilled out of the side of his mouth as he panted.

Mr Charles walked to the front of the group, holding on to Teddy's hand. Casey was sitting on the ground behind them with a book on her lap.

Mr Charles cleared his throat. "Excuse me, everybody! I just wanted to say a few things before we get started. Firstly, thank you for coming today. It's so wonderful to see so many of you here and for us all to work together for the good of the community.

"Now, if you don't mind, I'll organize you into groups. I thought one group could start at the back of the Rectory. Nina has asked if we wouldn't mind clearing some of the overgrown brambles that are creeping over the wall and into her lovely garden."

"We'll work there," said a woman from another street.

"Thank you!" said Mr Charles. "Sue, Claudia and Hannah, maybe you take some of the ivy off the main gates? Brian, could you start by strimming around the horse chestnut tree?"

"No problem," said Brian.

"Melody, Jake and Matthew, do you want to make a start over there?" Mr Charles pointed to the oldest area near the plague house.

"Mr Charles?" said Old Nina, quietly.

"Shouldn't some of the cemetery be left for wildlife? We don't want to drive any insects or other creatures away." I smiled. She was right. The graveyard was always full of butterflies, bumblebees and grasshoppers.

"Of course," said Mr Charles. "Just clear some of the pathways a little if you can, so that people can walk through without getting their legs scratched by thorns."

Old Nina smiled.

"Nina has kindly offered to serve the refreshments, so do pop back here for a cup of tea or coffee whenever you wish," said Mr Charles. "Teddy, Casey and I will come around to each of you with my wheelbarrow to collect the cuttings."

Teddy jumped up and down when he heard about the important job he'd be doing. Casey didn't look up from her book.

"Thank you, all!" Mr Charles said. "Your help with the Big Graveyard Clear-Up is greatly appreciated."

Everyone wandered off to their designated areas. Sue came over with a canvas bag with some tools and two pairs of gardening gloves for me and Jake. Matthew was already wearing a brand-new pair. He darted off towards Casey who was now standing up with her book under her arm. He crouched down in front of her and said something. She peered over his shoulder and glared at me. Then she looked back at Matthew and said something. They were talking about Dad's letter! I was sure of it!

Matthew came back.

"What was that all about?" I said.

"I'm just putting a few things in motion to get that letter for you, that's all," he said.

I smiled. He really was going to help!

The three of us headed off to where we'd been asked to work. Jake was being pulled in all directions as Wilson darted this way and that. It was like he didn't want to miss out on a chance to sniff *everything*.

Matthew and I walked past the water tap.

"I was thinking about you and Hal," he said. "Melody, have you ever thought that you might want to believe that Hal is telling the truth, because the alternative is too ... painful?" he said.

"What do you mean?" I said.

Matthew bit his bottom lip as he mulled over his words.

"You told me about your dad and how he'd been lying to you and your mum for so many years. I think you want Hal to be telling the truth so badly, that you're not seeing things straight. I wonder if you're being a little bit ... um ... gullible."

I thought about it for a bit.

"I don't know," I said. Thinking about it like that made me feel a bit dizzy. "Maybe it's got nothing to do with my dad. Maybe I choose to see the best in people and I like to give people a chance."

Matthew went quiet. We walked for a while in silence.

"Come on," he said. "Let's make a start."

We joined Jake, who was standing by some tall weeds that appeared to be moving on their own. Wilson suddenly appeared in the middle of them, his pure white fur now covered in green seeds.

"What do we do then?" said Jake.

"Clear some of these pathways I guess," I said. I bent down and pulled on a piece of ivy. I followed the vine as I pulled. It snaked along the path and on to a grave, where it had wrapped the now illegible headstone in a strangled grip. Tiny little suckers sprouted out all along its stem which held fast. I tugged hard and it eventually came free. I threw it on to the dusty path.

Matthew was standing watching. He probably didn't want to get too near to the graves as he was worried about germs.

"How about you snip the weeds and ivy into manageable pieces? It'll be easier for Mr Charles to collect if it's smaller," I said. I took some pruning shears from the canvas bag that Sue gave to me.

"Sure," he said, taking them.

I pulled on more of the ivy and Jake joined in as well. We both ended up with armfuls of long tendrils which we dropped beside Matthew. Jake kept Wilson's lead looped over his hand and every now and then he reached down and patted the little dog.

While we worked I thought about what Matthew had just said to me.

"Jake, do you think I'm gullible?" I said. Matthew shot me a look as Jake snorted.

"I guess," he said. "You're certainly unique, Melody. I don't think I've ever met anyone else like you."

I stopped and put my hands on my hips.

"What do you mean by that?" I said.

He turned to face me, wiping his forehead with the back of his hand.

"I dunno. I guess you can be a bit ... weird."

I scowled, ready to argue.

"But then you are kind and thoughtful too, so I guess that kind of makes up for the weird stuff."

I frowned at him. His eyes darted to mine then looked away again.

"It's like what you did in maths class the other day," he said. "When you stood up and said you'd thrown the eraser and then everyone copied you. That was typical Melody Bird." He began to laugh. "An odd thing to do but also ... nice."

He turned back to the weeds. I looked over at Matthew and he shrugged. I wasn't sure, but I think Jake Bishop had just given me a massive compliment.

I went back to pulling on the weeds. I thought that I would always have an odd friendship with Jake. He was so changeable: a bit like the wind. You never knew which direction he was going to blow in.

"I still can't understand why you're believing everything that Hal tells you, though," Jake piped up again.

I groaned.

"No, listen to me," he said. "Let's say he's telling the truth and trying to catch this so-called criminal, Martin Stone. What are those stupid notes all about? The riddles?"

A stinging nettle brushed against my shin and I felt a sharp, stinging pain. I crushed it beneath my trainer.

"Well, *someone* is leaving them," I said. "I picked up another one last night."

"What did it say?" said Matthew.

I stopped and wiped my forehead with my sleeve. There was no harm telling them now.

"It's definitely the hardest one yet," I said. "It says: *The man who made it did not want it; the man who bought it did not use it; the man who used it did not know it.*"

"That's just a load of nonsense," said Jake, brushing some dirt off his T-shirt. "What's the point of them?"

I shrugged. "Maybe it will make sense when I've put them all together."

I pulled on a thistle that nearly reached my waist, trying to avoid its sharp edges.

"*The man who used it did not know it,*" said Matthew, out loud. "What is it? Air? Oxygen?"

"No one makes oxygen though," said Jake, stopping for a moment. "And what about the man who bought it? That's well weird."

Jake turned his back and as he began to pull on a tall dandelion he stumbled back a little, on to the grave. "Urgh," he said, finding his balance. "The ground is all wonky here."

"That's where the coffins have rotted away," I said. "It makes the ground sink a little."

Jake shuddered then bent back to tackle the weed.

"Did you know they used to reuse coffins in Georgian times?" I said, remembering what Hal had told me. "They used to dig them up, tip out the bones and sell them again."

Matthew grimaced and Jake shook his head.

"See what I mean, Melody Bird? Weird," he said.

I pulled on some more ivy and stopped.

"Hang on a minute," I said. "The riddle! I think I've got it! *The man who used it did not know.* I clapped my hands together. "Oh, it's so brilliant!"

Matthew and Jake both grinned at me.

"Go on then. Tell us!" said Matthew. "What's the answer?"

I smiled at them both as they waited. Their

eyes were wide and eager to hear what the solution might be. My tummy tingled as I took a deep breath.

"It's a *coffin*," I said.

CHAPTER 34

"A coffin?" said Jake. "Why is it a coffin?"

"The man who made it did not want it!" said Matthew. "Of course he wouldn't want it. It's a coffin, after all!"

"And the man who bought it did not use it because, well, he was obviously buying it for someone else," I added.

"And the man who used it, did not know it ... because he was dead!" said Jake, grinning. He looked down at the grave and took a step to one side.

"Isn't it clever?" I said. Like with the other riddles, once you knew the answer it sounded so obvious.

"Does it make any sense with the other clues?" said Matthew.

I took my gardening gloves off and rubbed the side of my face.

"Let me think again," I said. "So, we have the mirror and the anchor. The gloves and ice."

"And now the coffin," said Jake.

We all thought about it for a minute.

"I don't get it," said Jake.

"Me neither," I said. "Do the objects have any connection at all?"

"Maybe it's an anagram of all the words put together," said Matthew.

"That's a lot of letters though, don't you think?" said Jake. "Unless it's a saying or a sentence. But how are you going to figure that out?"

The first letters of the words fluttered around my head like delicate little butterflies.

"Have either of you got a pen and paper with you?" I said.

"Er, no," said Jake.

I went over to a patch of dry dirt and picked up a stick.

"OK, so here's what we have," I said. I wrote out the words the best I could into the dirt.

Mirror
Anchor
Gloves
Ice
Coffin

Jake and Matthew stared at the words.

"Nope. Doesn't mean anything to me," said Jake.

"Hang on," said Matthew. "Could there be something in the order that they were left?"

I looked down at the words and then I saw it.

"There it is!" I said. "Look!"

I took my stick and circled the first letter of each word.

M
A
G
I
C

"Magic!" said Jake. "I see! Um, what does that mean then?"

"I don't know," I said. "I just don't know."

I was confused. This didn't sound like a message

from a criminal. I thought about Hal's trick with the disappearing pebbles. This felt like it had more to do with *Hal* than Martin Stone.

CHAPTER 35

"I've got to go!" I said.

I turned and ran off towards the main path. But when I reached it, I stopped. There was someone standing by the water tap.

Jake and Matthew arrived beside me, panting.

"Melody? What's going on?" said Matthew.

"Look!" I said. The man at the tap was filling his watering can. "That's him! The man with the gun. That's Martin Stone!"

Matthew froze.

"Shouldn't we go the other way? In case he sees us?" he said. He looked remarkably worried considering he apparently didn't believe anything

Hal had said.

"No," I said. "Let's just watch him for a moment."

Martin Stone stood still, his back slightly hunched as he waited for the can to fill up. I could see an outline of something pressing against the side of his jacket.

"The gun!" I whispered. "It's there!"

We all watched the man as he slowly began to twist the tap off. It made a horrible squeaking noise.

"What gun? I can't see anything," said Jake.

"It's in a holster under his jacket. We'll see it when he turns around," I said. But Martin Stone decided to take his jacket off. Slowly, he shook his arms out of the sleeves. Jake took a couple of steps forward, watching closely.

"Jake!" I said. "Don't go any closer!"

Martin Stone folded his jacket and placed it over his arm before reaching down for the watering can. We all saw it then – the brown, belted holster that was slung around his waist. I couldn't believe he was walking around with a gun, clearly on view! He turned around and began to walk towards us.

"Hang on a minute," said Jake. "That's Eddie Young! He works in the petrol garage."

"No!" I said. "That's Martin Stone!"

The man continued to head our way.

"And he hasn't got a gun!" said Jake. "It's a gardening tool!"

"What?" I said.

Martin Stone was coming closer and closer. When he was alongside us he nodded.

"Morning!" he said.

"Morning," we all mumbled back. I turned, just as he passed and this time, I saw exactly what was in the holster.

Jake was right, it wasn't a gun at all. It was a pair of small gardening clippers. Just like the pruning shears Matthew had been using to trim the ivy.

"Blimey," laughed Matthew. "I thought we were about to see bullets fly!"

Jake began to laugh as well.

My ears began to ring. They both found it *funny*. I had to get away from their laughter. I started to run. It felt like the graveyard was beginning to fold in on itself around me, the headstones like playing cards all collapsing in a row.

There were lies *everywhere*. First the riddles had spelled out the word "MAGIC" which meant absolutely *nothing*, Martin Stone was a man called Eddie, and now the gun wasn't a gun *at all*.

And Hal had been behaving all strangely earlier, pretending he didn't know who he was. Was that a part of his plan?

The realization hit me like a punch to the stomach. The shock took my breath away. Matthew was right. This was my worst nightmare and all that I'd been trying to avoid.

Hal was a fraud.

And I'd fallen for *everything*.

CHAPTER 36

Matthew and Jake caught up with me. "Are you OK, Melody?" said Matthew. "You're crying."

"Am I?" I said. I quickly wiped the tears from my face. I hadn't even realized.

I stood at the end of the alleyway, looking across at number one. "I just ... I just feel ... so stupid."

Jake and Matthew were quiet for a moment.

"Come on. Let's go and see what he's got to say for himself," said Jake.

"He won't be there," I said. I fumbled in my pocket for the key to number one. "Go and see for yourselves if you want," I said. "I don't need to."

There was no way Hal was going to be there

now. He knew Jake and Matthew were on to him, even if it had taken me a while to catch up. He would have made a run for it while we were all in the graveyard.

Jake took the key and they both walked up the path to number one. I crossed the road and sat down on our garden wall.

Hal wasn't a secret spy. There was no stakeout or Warley Tower branch or stolen Kingfisher Necklace. Everything was a lie.

A few minutes later, Matthew and Jake emerged from the house. They walked over to me.

"You're right, no sign of him," said Jake. "But he hasn't stolen anything."

"Everything is exactly how it was before he went in," said Matthew.

I felt exhausted.

"All OK over there?" It was Brian. He made his way down the alleyway towards us.

"Yes, Dad," said Matthew.

"Good, good," said Brian, brightly. "I've just popped back for some more milk for the tea break. Blimey. You three look miserable."

"Mr Corbin? Have you ever heard of MI8?" said Jake. I looked over at him. What was he doing?

"MI8? Well, I think it was a secret service agency a long time ago. But it doesn't exist any more," he said. "Why are you asking?"

"Someone told us he was working for MI8. He said he worked with the Warley branch or something. Where was it again, Melody?" he said to me.

"The Warley Tower branch," I said, sadly.

"Ah, well *that* exists," said Brian, smiling.

"It does?" said Matthew. "Who are they? What do they do?"

Brian laughed. "It's a place. Warley Tower. It's a block of flats at the end of the high street," he said. "Right, I'd better go and get this milk."

Brian went off to number nine and the three of us looked at each other. Was that where Hal had gone? To this Warley Tower block of flats?

"What do you reckon?" whispered Matthew. "It's worth checking out, don't you think?"

"Of course it is!" said Jake. "He can't go around telling Melody lies and taking her food and making her feel bad. It's not right!"

That made me feel a bit better. Although I still wasn't sure I wanted to face Hal.

"You were right, about what you said earlier,

Matthew," I said. "I *am* gullible. Why do I trust people so much?"

First Dad's lies and now this. It was so humiliating.

"I think *you* were right, Melody. You see the best in people and you're kind," said Matthew.

"And then look what happens! I get made to look *stupid*? It's not fair!" The tears began to roll down my face.

"Well, I'm going to have a word with him if you won't," said Jake. "Are you coming, Matthew?"

Matthew nodded. "Melody?" he said. "Are you going to come too?"

Jake and Matthew both looked very serious. Rather than laugh at me or make me feel silly, they were both angry that I'd been upset. It felt nice.

"OK," I said.

"Good," said Matthew. "Let's sort this out, once and for all."

"*And* I can get my clothes back!" said Jake.

CHAPTER 37

We walked to Warley Tower in silence for most of the way. Every now and then Jake and Matthew asked if I was OK. I just nodded.

I was trying to process everything that had happened and all the lies that Hal had told me; the riddles, Martin Stone, the broken "communication device", MI8, Special Agent Hal Vincent. It all felt so overwhelming. None of it was true? *None* of it?

Warley Tower was a grey-brick building with seven floors. I'd walked past it many times as it wasn't far from the town library, but I had never realized it had a name.

We stood by the glass entrance and looked up.

"Now what do we do?" said Matthew.

"Yeah, we can't just knock on every door," said Jake. "There must be over a hundred flats in there."

"Hold on," I said. "When you emptied Hal's rucksack there was an envelope in there. I thought it was for the MI8 office but it must be his home address."

"Brilliant! Can you remember what it said?" said Matthew.

Fortunately, I was good at memorizing things. And I'd had a lot of practice recently with the riddles.

"Yes. It said 408 Warley Tower," I said. "That must be the number of his flat."

"OK," said Jake. "Let's go then!"

We pushed open the double door and went in. The lift was out of order, so we went through another door to the stairs. The stairwell was freezing cold, even though it was warm outside. There was a strong smell of coffee in the air. Our footsteps echoed around the brick walls and eventually we came to another set of doors with a sign above them that said: FLOOR 4.

"408 must be along here somewhere," I said. I pushed the doors open and we walked along the corridor until we came to number 408. The door was brown. I felt strange. Hal had lied to me. Did I really want to see him again?

"I'm not sure about this," I said. I looked at Matthew and Jake. My heart was pounding. Facing Hal could make things worse. He might start laughing at me and I didn't think I could cope with that: Melody Bird – what a fool!

"Let's just see if anyone's there," said Jake. Before I had a chance to object, he stepped forward and banged on the door with his fist.

As his knuckles hit against the wood, the door creaked open. It hadn't been shut properly. Jake looked at me and Matthew, then pushed it open further with his foot. We peered inside.

The door opened on to a small, square hallway. The carpet was grey and the walls were covered with brown-striped wallpaper. There was a small table on one side with nothing on it. On the carpet was a pile of post.

"Hello? Is anyone there?" shouted Jake. He went in.

"Jake!" I said, through clenched teeth. "What are you doing?"

"I'm seeing if anyone's home, that's the point of

us being here, isn't it?" he said. Matthew followed. I hesitated for a moment, then went in too. I picked up the post and looked to see who they were addressed to: H Vincent, Ms H Vincent, Helen Vincent – they all seemed to be for one person. I put the post back on the table.

On the left was a door which was shut. We walked ahead and into a lounge.

"There's no TV," said Jake, looking around. "Who doesn't have a TV in their living room? And it's so . . . empty."

The room was very bare. There was just a dark-brown sofa, a wooden chair with a single cream cushion on the seat and an electric fire. There were no ornaments or photographs or pictures or books. On the windowsill was a pair of binoculars. Matthew went to the window.

He turned to us, a shocked look on his face.

"Come and see this," he said.

Jake and I went over. The window looked down on to the busy high street. I watched as the tops of people's heads went in and out of shops. Four people stood waiting at a bus stop.

"Good view," said Jake.

"No, you don't understand!" said Matthew.

"Look at that door between the hairdressers and the coffee shop."

On the opposite side of the road between the two buildings and not far from the bus stop was a single, glass door.

"Yeah, I see it," said Jake. "What about it?"

"That's Dr Rhodes's office!" said Matthew. "That's where I go on Mondays for my appointments. Remember how Hal knew all those things about me? What time I was there, when I talked to that kid and woman at the bus stop? He can see it all happening from here!"

I picked up the binoculars and held them to my eyes, adjusting the focus. Beside the door was a brass sign and a buzzer. I could just make out what it said:

1st Floor. Psychotherapist – Dr Rhodes

I put them back down and Jake grabbed them from me, taking a look.

"Yep," he said. "He had the best view from here, that's for sure."

"But why?" said Matthew. He looked shaken. "If MI8 isn't real then why was he watching me?"

"Let's check out the rest of the flat," said Jake. We went back to the hallway and he opened the closed door.

It was a bedroom. In the centre was a double bed, neatly made, with a plain, pale-blue duvet. On one side of the bed was a small, white table with a lamp and a glass of water. In the corner was a brown wardrobe. Again, the room felt really sparse. On the bedside table were some foil packets that looked like some kind of medication. There were were no photographs or books. It felt eerie, and wrong to be in someone's private room.

"Come on," I said. "We shouldn't be here. Let's just go home."

But Jake turned and walked off. Matthew and I followed him into a kitchen. There was a cooker with four rings, a sink, and a small table. Beside the table were two folded chairs. On the kitchen worktop was a small box-shaped fridge, humming quietly.

"Come on, Jake. Melody's right. Let's go," said Matthew. "This place gives me the creeps."

"But we haven't looked everywhere yet," said Jake. There were two more doors leading off the hallway. One open, one shut. I checked the open door. Through it was a peach-coloured bathroom. Then I stood in front of the other closed door and took a deep breath.

"What do you think, Matthew?" I said, quietly. "Should we go in?"

Matthew shrugged. I took a deep breath, turned the handle and stepped inside.

This room was completely different. For a start, it was full of colour. The plain walls were decorated with posters which instantly made it feel more like a home. I looked around and then gasped. There was a boy, curled up on the bed.

It was Hal. He was laying on his side with his arms hugging his knees. He looked very small and very frightened.

"Hal? It's us. Are you OK?" I said. I felt my anger subside a little. There was something going on here that I was yet to understand. Matthew and Jake stepped into the room behind me.

"Is he dead?" whispered Jake.

"Of course he's not dead," Matthew whispered back.

Hal was just staring into space. I'd seen him like this twice now; that day in the plague house where he seemed to have lost all sense of where he was and earlier today when the watch was smashed.

"I think he's in shock," I said. "That's when the brain gets overloaded and shuts down for a bit."

I looked around the room. Above the bed was a giant poster of a man in a dark suit with a loose tie hanging around his neck. He held his arms up against his chest as he stared back at us. Beside him, in big red letters, were the words:

JAMES BOND IS BACK

There was a desk in the corner and I walked over to it. There was a pot filled with pens and pencils and a wall calendar dated 2005. There was also a pile of old comics dating back twenty years. The comic on the top had some bright yellow wording on the cover:

Fiendishly Fun Riddles To Solve!
(Turn to page 7)

I flicked through the pages and stopped.

Can you solve these mind-bending riddles?
Take the first letter of each answer to spell out an *enchanting* word!

(Answers in next week's edition!)

1) Use me wisely and I am somebody,
   Turn me round and I am nobody.
2) When you use me, you throw me away.
   When you're finished with me, you
   take me in.

What am I?

They were all there – all of the riddles that had been hidden in the graveyard! *This* was where Hal must have got the idea from. They had been taken *from a comic*! I raced through the rest of the pile, throwing them to the side.

"Melody? Are you OK?" said Matthew. I ignored him.

In amongst the pile were three magazines titled *The Ten Most Famous!* I looked at the covers.

The Ten Most Famous World Disasters!
The Ten Most Famous Victorians!
The Ten Most Famous Thefts!

I picked up this last one. I turned to the contents.

I spotted it straight away.

Pg 17 Kingfisher Necklace theft.

On page 17 was a photograph of a beautiful necklace, studded with jewels of different colours: blue, orange, green. Underneath it read:

Kingfisher Necklace c1877

I read the beginning of the article, which was similar to what I had read on the internet.

The Kingfisher Necklace was stolen in the dead of night from the Fitzwilliam Museum in January, 2015. The necklace has never been seen since and no progress has been made to discover the identity of the criminals involved. Police believe the necklace was stolen to order and...

I looked at Jake and Matthew.
"Everything he ever told me is here," I said. "*Everything.*" My stomach churned and I started to feel sick. There were two books on the desk. One was a children's encyclopaedia which had a picture

of Albert Einstein on the cover. I picked up the other book.

"Look. *Easy Tricks for the Amateur Magician*," I read out loud. I traced the front with my finger. "Written by ... *Martin Stone*," I said. I dropped the book on to the floor. I felt a wave of anger as I looked at the boy, lying motionless on the bed.

"Was this your idea of fun?" I said to him. "You magpied a story, didn't you?"

Matthew took a step towards me. "Melody, calm down," he said, softly.

I pushed past him and stood inches from Hal. His back rose and fell but he stayed silent.

"This is where it all came from, isn't it?" I shouted, waving my hand around his room. "The riddles, the Kingfisher Necklace, Martin Stone? You stole the bits you wanted ... like a magpie. And then you made it all up!"

I turned and looked up at the poster of James Bond. He was staring at me with one eyebrow raised and an amused look on his face.

"*And* you pretended to be a spy!" I said. I felt tears beginning to fill my eyes. "It was all just a game to you, wasn't it? Did you think it was funny to lie to me like that? To make me look *stupid*?"

Very slowly, Hal turned on to his back and stared at the ceiling. In his hands he was still holding the broken pieces of watch. Then he began to speak.

"It was how I passed the time," he said. "By making up stories."

Jake looked confused. "What do you mean 'passed the time'?" he said. "You make it sound like you've been in prison."

Hal turned his head sharply. "It's not a prison," he said. "This is my home."

"Who lives here with you, Hal?" said Matthew.

Hal slowly raised his arms and put them over his face. "My mum," he said, his voice muffled. "But she wasn't well. And now she's gone."

Matthew, Jake and I looked at each other.

"What happened to her?" said Matthew.

Hal put his arms down, wiping his eyes with his fingers.

"For some of the time, Mum was OK. We'd play games and read books together. But there were other times when she was scared. She used to look out of the window with her binoculars. She said we were being watched. Sometimes she would stay up all night, just looking out on to the street. She said she wanted to protect me. She said that the world was a dangerous place and that we needed to stay inside," he said. "She said ... she said that there were bad people who would take me away if I was seen."

Matthew took a step forward. "What bad people?" he said.

Hal paused for a moment and took a few long breaths. "Criminals," said Hal. "She said that they were everywhere and to be safe we had to stay inside as much as possible. We both kept an eye on the street, using the binoculars, watching for them. Making sure they weren't coming."

Matthew nodded. "That's when you saw me, wasn't it? Going to my appointments."

Hal nodded. "When I saw you in the plague house I recognized you immediately. I'd seen you going through that door every Monday at five p.m. for one hour." Hal pushed himself up to a seated position. "I didn't mean any harm, Matthew," he said. "I'm sorry."

Matthew just nodded. He knew what that felt like; to watch the world from your window.

"So, your mum wasn't well and she thought that there were bad people out there trying to get you?"

said Jake. Hal nodded.

As I listened, I felt my anger begin to evaporate. This sounded awful.

"And you had to stay inside a lot?" I said. Hal swallowed a few times and stared down at the carpet.

"All the time," he said.

None of us spoke for a moment.

Then Jake said, "What do you mean, all the time?"

Hal didn't reply.

"What about your teachers? Your friends? Your family? A doctor?" said Matthew. "Haven't they helped you?"

"You don't understand, Matthew. I don't have any teachers. I don't have friends, I have no family. I've never been to a doctor." Hal looked up.

"Nobody knows I exist," he said.

CHAPTER 38

We stood there, utterly stunned. No one knew he existed? How could that be true?

"I'll put the kettle on," said Jake.

"What?" said Matthew.

Jake shrugged. "That's what adults do in times like this, don't they? Put the kettle on?"

"I like tea," said Hal, smiling weakly. Jake seemed pleased to have something to do and he headed off to the kitchen. We could hear him rattling around in the cupboards and filling the kettle.

"Where's your mum now, Hal?" I said. He took a deep breath before he answered.

"She got ill. I don't mean in her head, although that was bad enough. This time it was her stomach. She was screaming in pain and it just got worse and worse. I think it might have been appendicitis. I made her call for an ambulance and they came and took her away." His voice wavered and he paused for a moment. "When they were here, I hid in the wardrobe. The paramedics asked her if she lived on her own and she said yes. She was just trying to protect me. From the criminals."

Matthew looked at me, his face looked so worried it made me feel frightened.

"She didn't come back," Hal continued. "I worried that the police or the ambulance people were going to find me and I'd get Mum in trouble. I didn't know what to do, so I packed a bag and left. I hadn't been outside in so long I was frightened at first. I used to go for walks with my mum, until she decided it was too dangerous. I'd forgotten how fast everything is. And how loud!" He smiled, but it faded quickly. "I walked and walked and then I found the church near your road. I sat in there for hours, just looking at the sunlight flickering through the windows. It was so nice, so peaceful. There was nobody telling me to be scared any more."

Jake appeared with a mug.

"The milk's gone off, I'm afraid. But I put some sugar in it like you do for people in shock," he said.

I smiled at him.

Hal sipped the black tea, then carried on.

"I had a walk around the churchyard and then I found the plague house. It was perfect. Secluded. Covered with overgrowth. I didn't think *anyone* would find me there. But Melody Bird did."

"And why didn't you just tell me the truth?" I said. "Why make up the whole story about MI8 and staking out Martin Stone?"

Hal stared at his knees.

"I'm sorry, Melody Bird. I know it's hard to believe but . . . but I didn't feel like I *was* lying," he said. "It all felt so . . . real."

I thought back to how he acted when I first met him. He really did seem to be living as if he was a spy – not making up a story on the spot.

"It was like a survival mechanism I guess," said Matthew. "It gave you a purpose?"

Hal nodded. "You enjoyed solving the riddles, didn't you, Melody Bird?" He looked at me. "You said you felt lonely and I thought it would be nice for you to be included. I'm sorry it wasn't real."

I glanced at Matthew and Jake, who looked a bit embarrassed about Hal calling me lonely.

"It's fine," I said, holding my head high. "I solved the last one too! It was a coffin wasn't it? And the objects spelled out 'magic'. It was brilliant."

Hal smiled. He looked so tired.

"What do we do now then?" said Jake. "We can't just leave him here."

"Hal, we need to tell someone about what's happened," said Matthew. "Then we can find out where your mum is."

Hal looked frightened.

"No. I can't let her down. I promised her I'd stay hidden. She'll be so upset!" he said.

"But your mum is unwell," I said, putting my hand on his shoulder. "I don't mean the appendicitis, I mean in her head. I expect that's why she hasn't come home. They're probably keeping her safe and trying to help her."

Hal chewed on his bottom lip and then he looked up at me. "Can I come and stay with you?" he said. "Or you, Jake? Or you, Matthew?" He looked at each of us in turn. "You're the only friends I have."

The three of us looked at each other. We all knew this would be unlikely.

"We'll see, shall we?" I said. "Let's just go back to my house and talk to my mum and we'll go from there."

Hal let out a sigh.

"Thank you, Melody Bird," he said.

He sounded relieved, as if everything was going to be all right now. Unfortunately, I wasn't quite so sure.

CHAPTER 39

We got to Chestnut Close just as everyone was coming back from the Big-Clear Up. Mum, Sue and Sheila were heading towards us.

"Where have you all been?" said Sue. "Brian said you'd all gone off to town."

"What's going on, Melody?" Mum said. She looked at Hal and then back at us.

I suddenly felt like I wanted to curl up into her arms. Hearing about Hal's mum had been so upsetting.

"Melody?" she said. She looked worried.

"Mum. This is Hal. I really need to talk to you," I said. She saw my face and immediately held out her arms. I walked over and rested my cheek against her chest as she wrapped her arms around me and stroked my hair. I bit my lip as I saw Hal watching. I was so lucky, to have my mum right here.

"Let's go in and put the kettle on, shall we?" she said. I smiled at Jake and he raised his eyebrows in a "told you so" way.

"Sue? Sheila? Do you fancy a cuppa?" said Mum. "I think these three might have something to tell us. Hal, why don't you join us?"

He smiled and nodded and we all headed towards my house.

There was a rumbling sound as Mr Charles emerged from the alleyway pushing Teddy in a wheelbarrow. Teddy was holding on to the sides with a big grin on his face. Casey was following them, dragging a large green canvas bag full of garden tools. She was red in the face and looked very, very fed up. Just then a shiny black car drove on to the close.

"It's Mummy!" called Teddy. He waved madly as the car pulled up outside number eleven. It looked like Melissa Dawson was back to collect her children.

Matthew stopped.

"I'll be back in a minute," he said to me.

"Let me help you with that, Casey!" he said, taking the heavy bag and putting it over his shoulder. He looked up at me and gave me a wink. My stomach turned over. Dad's letter! He was still going to try and get it for me.

When we got home, I told Mum, Sue and Sheila all about finding Hal in the plague house. I saw Mum press her lips together. I'm sure she was shocked that I hadn't said any of this to her.

I told them that Hal said he worked for MI8 and was investigating a stolen necklace and staking out a known criminal. I told them that we'd moved him to number one so he wouldn't be found, and then the revelation that we'd only just discovered ourselves: that it was all made up and he had nowhere to go.

I left them in the lounge, talking quietly. I could hear the words "police" and "social workers".

Hal was in the kitchen sitting by Frankie's bed, gently stroking his back. He hadn't said much, apart to confirm his address to Mum and say that his own mum was called Helen Vincent. I switched the kettle on for more tea.

"What do you think is going to happen to him?" I whispered to Jake. "Matthew's mum is talking about phoning the police." Fortunately, Hal couldn't hear us over the boiling kettle.

"I guess they'll get social services involved," he said. "They'll know what to do." I put some mugs on to the kitchen counter and then Mum came in.

"Why didn't you talk to me, Melody?" she said. "I could have helped you. And Hal."

We all looked at him but he seemed to be more interested in Frankie's velvet ears than listening to us.

"I'm sorry, Mum," I said. She gave my arm a squeeze but I could see the hurt on her face.

"I just can't believe *no one* knows he exists," said Jake. "It's mad! What about when he was born?" He turned around. "Hal, do you know when your birthday is?"

"Twelfth of September," said Hal, not looking up. "I was born in the flat fifteen years ago. Mum said she was all on her own at the time."

"Surely *someone* knew he had been born," I said. "What about his vaccinations? When he got ill?"

Jake shrugged his shoulders. "I guess his mum

was so determined, she made it happen," he said.

Mum poured the boiling water on to the teabags and I got the milk out of the fridge.

"Melody Bird's mum?" said Hal. "Will I be staying with you or with Jake or Matthew?" He suddenly seemed to have lost about ten years in age.

"Let's just see what happens, shall we?" said Mum, brightly. "We need to make a few phone calls first. Do you want anything to eat? Some soup? A chocolate brownie?"

The plastic tub from the Big Graveyard Clear-up was on the side with one solitary brownie left inside.

"What's a brownie?" said Hal, looking confused.

"Have you never eaten one before?" said Jake. He grinned and grabbed the tub, pulling the lid off with a *pop*. "You are in for a treat. These are incredible! And nut-free, too."

Hal smiled and took the brownie. His smile expanded even more when he had a bite. Mum took the tray of teas into the living room and I followed.

"Someone from the station is coming over now," said Sheila. "And social services are sending someone too."

"Melody, love," said Mum. "You know Hal can't stay here, don't you?"

I felt a lump forming in my throat.

"I know," I said. "It's just… I'm his only friend in the world. What is he going to do?"

When the police and social worker arrived, Mum told me that Jake needed to go home and that I should wait in my room. I sat on my bed, trying to listen to what was going on downstairs, but all I could hear were muffled voices.

Mum came up at six o'clock to say that Hal was leaving and that I could go downstairs and say goodbye. She said that he was going into temporary foster care until the whereabouts of his mum could be established.

"And what if she's too unwell? What if they can't find her?" I said.

"I don't know, darling," she said. "I guess he'll stay in foster care."

"We could look after him if we don't move!" I said. "We've got a spare room. He can go to my school. He is so nice, Mum. You'd really like him!"

Mum sighed. "I'm sure I would, Melody. But

it's just not allowed. We're strangers, not family."

She reached out and put her hand on my shoulder. "Come on. Come downstairs and say goodbye," she said.

I could feel tears building up behind my eyes. I really didn't want to cry in front of Hal. I wanted him to leave feeling safe and that everything was going to be all right.

Hal was standing by the door, his rucksack over his shoulder.

"It looks like I'm not staying here after all, Melody Bird," he said. His face was crumpled with a frown. "They're ... they're taking me to someone's house. Apparently, they are a very nice couple."

I could tell he was really nervous.

"I'm sorry, Hal," I said. "I'm sorry you can't stay here. It's not allowed."

He dropped his gaze. A small tear escaped through the crease of his eye.

"I'm sorry I lied to you," he said. "I don't think I even realized I was doing it."

I smiled.

"You'll make a brilliant author one day, Hal," I said. My throat caught and I let out a small sob.

It was enough to make me start crying.

"It has been a pleasure to know you, Hal," I said.

Hal looked up and smiled through his own tears.

"I have enjoyed every single second of being in your company, Melody Bird," he said. And then he turned and went through the door.

CHAPTER 40

The morning after Hal left our doorbell rang.

"Can you get that, Melody?" called Mum from the back garden. She had just got our lawnmower out of the shed and was about to cut the grass.

I opened the door. It was Matthew. And he had a white envelope in his hand.

"You got it!" I said. My hand was shaking when I took it.

"It was easy!" said Matthew. "Mr Charles was distracted with Melissa turning up and Teddy just wanted his mum. Earlier, in the graveyard, I told Casey that if she got it for me, the next time she came to stay I'd get her a present, whatever she wanted. She passed it over the back fence after we got back last night. I didn't want to bring it over, what with everything that was going on with Hal."

"Thank you!" I said. I held the envelope tightly to my chest. "What was it that she asked for?" I dreaded to think.

"That's the thing," said Matthew. "She didn't want *anything*. She said that instead of a present, could she come to my house and have dinner and do jigsaws with me."

"Really?" I said. "That's it?"

Matthew nodded.

"She had one other request. She was to come on her own, without Teddy. Do you know, I think she just wants some attention."

I looked at the letter in my hand and Matthew followed my gaze.

"Thank you, Matthew," I said. "It really means a lot that you've helped me."

Matthew nodded.

"Good luck, Melody. I hope there's everything in there that you wish for," he said.

I closed the door and walked into the lounge. Mum was sitting in the armchair reading a book.

"Who was that, Melody?" said Mum.

"Matthew," I said. I held out the envelope.

Mum looked at the handwriting and her face dropped.

"Oh my goodness," she said.

"Let's read it together, shall we?" I said.

We started at the beginning, where Dad told Mr Charles how he'd made a mess of everything, and then we got to the part I hadn't managed to read.

> What I wanted to ask you is this. Would you be able to look out for Claudia and Melody for me? If you could check in on them now and then I would be so grateful.
>
> I've sent a few letters in the past but I suspect they've never been read, which is understandable. I've tried to call but Claudia has changed her mobile number and I'm concerned that if I just turn up at the house I'd be causing more anguish.
>
> There is no need for you to tell them about our arrangement. I appreciate that they don't want any contact from me and this is a decision I will have to learn to live with.

The letter went on to say that he realized he made a bad choice in agreeing to cut all contact with us, but at the time he thought that it would be better for us if he just disappeared from our lives. This worked for a while, but the reality was that he missed me and he'd ruined his chance of being my dad. He knew he'd never be forgiven, but he hoped that Mr Charles would let him know if we ever needed anything. He signed the letter: *A failed father.*

We both cried when we got to the end and Mum gave me a big hug. "It's true, Melody," she said. "He did write to us for a while, but I destroyed the letters without reading them. After a while they stopped coming."

"That's OK, Mum," I said. "I understand."

We stared at the phone number at the top of the letter.

"What do you want me to do?" Mum said. "Shall I call?"

I thought about all the times I'd felt like I hated my dad. But then there were just as many times when I had wished I could talk to him. He might have treated us incredibly badly, but I still missed him.

"I think you should call him, Mum," I said. "He's not a part of Team MC and he never will be, but he's still my dad."

Mum slowly nodded, then she stood up and took her mobile phone out of her pocket and made her way to the garden.

CHAPTER 41

After Hal left, we still had a couple of months to go until the summer holidays. The days dragged on and on and then, suddenly, we had six weeks stretching before us.

On the first Saturday we had off I helped Mum and Erica in the organic café. I worked in the kitchen, washing up and chopping vegetables. I absolutely loved it. I was going to try and earn enough money to buy a camera. I wanted to take lots of black-and-white photographs of the cemetery and make a collage for my bedroom wall.

When I got home after my first shift I had a long, hot shower. It was tiring being on my feet all day, but I was buzzing with the feeling of having earned my very first wage packet. I got dry and changed into my black jeans and a grey top.

Mum called up to the bathroom.

"Melody! Matthew and Jake are here!"

I pulled my hair back into a hairband and made my way downstairs.

Jake and Matthew stood on the doorstep with Wilson sitting by Jake's feet. Behind Matthew I could see the large SOLD sign that loomed over the street.

"It's sold then?" I said.

"Yep," said Jake. "Hannah texted Mum last week. Apparently, Mr Jenkins has agreed to get help with his anger issues and they are going to have a fresh start in another town somewhere. Hopefully it'll be miles away from here."

None of us had seen Mr Jenkins since the showdown in the school car park. After the Big Graveyard Clear-up, Hannah moved back with her parents. Before she went she asked Sue if she wouldn't mind looking after Wilson as it would be too much to take him as well. Because his breed was anti-allergy and Jake wouldn't react, Sue said yes.

"And what about Wilson?" I said. "Is he going back to the Jenkins's now?"

Jake smiled and shook his head. "Nope. I get to keep the annoying, fluffy wig after all," he said. I thought Jake must be doing a good job looking after Wilson. He was very well behaved now and we never saw him barking on the windowsill in his house. Jake said it was because he gave him lots of attention.

Mum came and joined us from the kitchen.

"This came in the post earlier, Melody," she said. In her hand was a brown envelope. "I thought you might want to open it with your friends."

I looked down at the address on the envelope. I rarely got any post apart from birthday cards. The address read:

Super-spy Melody Bird and Frankie the
sausage dog,
3 Chestnut Close

"Oh," I said. I swallowed. I knew exactly who it was from.

"Have a nice walk, you three," said Mum.

"We will," smiled Matthew.

I put the envelope in my pocket and Frankie on his lead and we stepped outside.

Our walk around the graveyard had become a weekly event. I'd take Frankie, Jake would take Wilson and Matthew would come too.

"Is the letter from him?" said Matthew. We came out of the alleyway into the dappled sunlight.

"It must be. The handwriting looks identical to the riddles. And who else would call me a super-spy?" I smiled, but inside I was really nervous. How had Hal's life changed since we last saw him? Was he happy? Had they found his mum? It had been so long since they'd taken him away. A lot could have happened in that time.

"I'll open it in a minute," I said, quietly. Matthew nodded and started talking about the holiday he was going on with his mum and dad to the Lake District. It would be the first holiday they'd had in years because of his OCD.

"You are so lucky," said Jake. "I think we're going to Auntie Wendy's caravan again. It's so *boring*. There's nothing to do there apart from bingo with a load of old people."

Matthew and I laughed.

"How about you, Melody? Are you going away this summer?" said Matthew.

I shook my head. "No." We couldn't afford it. "But I might get a visit from my dad."

"Oh wow, has he been in touch?" said Matthew.

"Yes. Mum speaks to him every few weeks now. He has been asking to see me and I think I'm ready," I said. "He's been helping out with money too."

The FOR SALE sign that had stood outside of our house was gone, Mum had agreed to accept financial help from Dad for six months, and then she said she'd "assess the situation". She'd also had a long chat with Mr Charles when she took Dad's letter back to him. Mr Charles used to work in finance and said he was happy to offer her any advice she might need. She said she might take him up on that one day.

We got to the big horse chestnut tree with the circular bench.

"OK. I'm going to read it now," I said. "Maybe on my own first."

Matthew and Jake held back as I made my way to the tree and sat down. Frankie lay down at my feet. I took the envelope out of my pocket and slowly opened it. Inside was a folded letter and a photograph, which I put to one side.

Dear Melody

I'm sorry that it has taken me so long to write to you, but life has been particularly busy since I last saw you.

After I left your house I was placed with some foster carers who looked after me for many weeks. They were nice enough, but I did feel lonely.

Janet, my social worker, kept in touch with me and after a few days she told me they'd managed to trace Mum. She was living in a special hospital where the doctors were trying to make her head better, although it was taking a long time. Apparently, she'd been talking about me but because there was no record of me existing, no one believed her. They thought I was just part of her mind playing tricks on her.

I went with Janet to see her at the hospital. There were nurses there too and someone taking notes. I didn't like it at all. Mum kept crying. I don't think I was helping her by being there.

The good news is that it turns out I have a family! And a big one at that. Mum has a brother called Jeff and he has a wife called Clare. Janet contacted them and when they found out I existed they offered to look after me. It took a very, very long time for it to be agreed, but three weeks ago I moved out of the foster home and in with them.

Jeff and Clare are really nice. I've shown them all of the magic tricks that I know and Jeff has taught me a few more. They have a son called Albie but he's on a gap year from university and travelling around Europe so I've only seen photos of him so far. He's my cousin, I guess!

I'm starting school in September and I am really, really scared. But I suppose that's normal. If you have any tips, I'd really appreciate them.

Jeff and Clare are in touch with the hospital where Mum is staying and the doctors say she's improving, but that it will take time. She might come out of hospital one day and when she does I might be able to visit her with Janet. Clare said I mustn't worry about it right now.

Tell Matthew I've been seeing a therapist who is a bit like the one he sees! He's called Mark and he helps me to understand my feelings and to try and make sense of it all. I told him all about MI8 and he said it was my brain's way of coping with a very stressful situation. Like a survival mechanism. He said that I had created a world that felt safe to me, but it was all in my head. My watch was my link with my mum and when that got smashed, it was like the spell was broken and that's why I was so confused for a while. Anyway, I hope you can forgive me. I didn't mean to lie.

I hope that Matthew and Jake are well. And say hello to Frankie for me, too. I have an address so you can write back if you like! You're a true friend, Melody Bird.

Yours,
Hal

I lifted up the photograph. It was of three people standing on a shingle beach. Hal was in the centre, wearing a chunky, navy jumper. His face was wide with a big smile and his cheeks were flushed from the sea air. On either side of him were two adults who I guessed must have been Clare and Jeff, his aunt and uncle. They were grinning too. Behind them, I could see the white froth of a wave crashing on to the beach.

When I looked up, Matthew and Jake had walked over and were sitting either side of me. I folded the letter and put it back into the envelope, along with the photograph. Frankie sat down beside my foot and pressed his warm body against my leg. I reached down and gently stroked his soft head.

"Well?" said Jake. "What did he say?"

I took a long deep breath as I looked around at the beautiful graveyard. I was so incredibly grateful that I didn't have to move away from the place I loved. I was also grateful for the two friends sitting beside me and for my other friend, Hal, living just a letter away.

"Come on, Melody," said Matthew. "How is he?"

I looked at them both and I smiled.

"He's absolutely fine," I said.

Also by
LISA THOMPSON

A story of finding friendship when you're lonely, and hope when all you feel is fear.

"A great cast of characters and an intriguing mystery – I loved it!"
Ross Welford, bestselling author of *Time Travelling with a Hamster*

A story of finding friendship
and the strength to light up the dark.

"*Pure, breathtaking genius*"
Maz Evans, bestselling author
of *Who Let the Gods Out*

A story of family, friendship and finding your place in the world.

"Brimming with Thompson's characteristic warmth and wisdom"
The Bookseller

What if your little white lie made you famous?
A story of fame and fortune, making mistakes
and learning to be true to yourself.

"Thompson's writing is full of heart, warmth and
humour and she's not afraid to address thought-
provoking questions about the illusion of wealth
and what it means to be happy."
The Bookseller